To Meg
from
the three
of us.
1985

3
THE CAMEO SERIES

Katharine's Yesterday

GRACE LIVINGSTON HILL

Tyndale House
Publishers, Inc.
Wheaton, Illinois

Katharine's Yesterday was originally published
by the Lothrop Publishing Company in 1895.

First printing, August 1984

Library of Congress Catalog Card Number 84-50540
ISBN 0-8423-2029-6, cloth
Copyright © 1984 by Robert L. Munce Publishing Co.
All rights reserved
Printed in the United States of America

CONTENTS

KATHARINE'S YESTERDAY

I. SUMMER'S END

KATHARINE Bowman stood at the front gate of her father's house, looking drearily down the road at nothing in particular. The air was crisp and clear, and the sunshine of the early morning was making everything dance and sparkle. All the brilliant red leaves, with their dew-covered faces, came fluttering down with a frosty air. They clanked and clattered against one another, as if to pretend that fall was well on its way and winter would soon be here. Nothing could have looked more enticing that October morning; the air, the sunshine, the leaves, and the very grass seemed full of delightful possibilities. Katharine saw them all: the little whirls of white dust down the road; the purple and blue mists on the distant hills at the end of the street; the big hill, or "mountain" as it was called, which loomed up before her just across the meadows. She had climbed it in company with a party of young people only a few days before. A little brisk black-and-tan dog moved along the sidewalk in a lively manner, and the cheerful little sparrows that hopped in the road did not care whether winter came or not, but none of them gave Katharine any pleasure or sense of joy.

The truth was, the world looked pretty dark to her that morning. She had just come from the depot, where she had watched the morning express whizz out of sight, carrying with it half a dozen young people, who had been all in all to her the whole summer. They had played tennis and croquet together, had read and sung, walked and talked, gone on picnics, taken rides, and, in short, done all the delightful things that a party of congenial, bright young people can think up to do during a long summer in a country village.

The last delegation of them had gone away this morning; and now only Katharine was left, surrounded by all the pleasant places where they had enjoyed themselves together. How dreary they looked to her now. What was that great hill now, with its waving scarlet foliage and its stores of autumn brilliance? Nothing but a hill, which she would not climb alone. What was the tennis court, with its clean-shaven smoothness and its clear, white lines, over which played the mirthful sunshine and occasionally a yellow-and-brown leaf? Nothing but a desolate reminder of happy days all gone.

Yes, the summer was over and the winter had begun, a whole long winter, full of work and disagreeableness. She remembered the old brown cashmere dress that lay on her table this morning. Her mother had put it there, reminding her that it should be ripped, sponged, and pressed, to be made over. How she hated made-over things! She glanced down at the stylish street suit she had on. It would have to be put away and kept only for special occasions, now that there was no more company. Her pretty tennis suit, too, would have no use. Then there was a pile of mending, that had been accumulating during the months when she had given herself over to good times. What else was there not to be done, day in and day out, this long, barren winter?

In the house a pile of dishes was awaiting her attention. The servant had gone away for a day or two, and Katharine knew that the dishes would be left until she returned from the station, as her mother was very busy with the dressmaker. Still she lingered at the gate, dreading to go in and begin the winter. She thought miserably of the other happy girls who had left her, some to spend their winters in boarding school, others in their city homes, and the young men, most of them in college or at their business. It must be so nice, she thought, to be in business, and not have to poke at home and wash dishes. She wished she could go to school this winter. Why was it that her father's business could not have been as good this particular winter, just when she would have so enjoyed going to the seminary with Mabel and Fannie?

She drew a long sigh, and turned away from the gate, drawing off her gloves as she moved slowly toward the house. She would not look at the tennis court as she passed it, and two tears slipped out and rolled down her cheeks. She did so love tennis, and now there would be no more until next summer. Of course, she could not play alone.

But once in the house there was plenty to be done, and no one else there seemed to have time to think of yesterday.

"Katharine, I wish you would wash the dishes as soon as possible, and then make a cake. Mrs. Whiting is coming down to tea tonight and to go to prayer meeting, and there isn't a bit of cake in the house. Make the easiest, quickest kind, and get through as soon as possible. There is a great deal to be done, and I shall need your help this morning." Her mother said this as she entered the door.

Yesterday, when Katharine had been playing tennis, Frank Warner, her partner, had watched her several times. He had thought what a pleasant expression she always had, and what an exceedingly nice girl she was, for a girl who had been brought up in a small village, and whose father had never been able to give her many advantages. But he would scarcely have known her if he could have seen her now as she took off her hat and jacket, with an almost sullen expression on her face, and her brows drawn together in an inartistic scowl.

There was no time for her to examine the package that the girls had given to her at parting, and which she had not had the heart to open before, so she laid it on the table to wait until a leisure moment should come.

It seemed to her as though the task of washing all

those sticky, ugly looking dishes was an impossible one, and likely to prove interminable. She made it all the harder for herself by continually envisioning pleasant things that had happened the days before, and discontentedly wishing those days back once more.

The work of getting the dinner fell mostly upon her shoulders that day, and it was performed very reluctantly. She scowled at everything, and sighed until her brother John told her she sounded like a steam engine. She told him in reply that he was a saucy, unbrotherly fellow. Then she went to work to make a pudding for dinner which she knew he did not like, just because it took less time than others which he did like; and things did not matter to her much, anyway, that day. Her heart was all in the past summer, mourning for it and its joys as one does for a dead friend.

Dinner was over at last, and the dishes washed; but there was no rest nor leisure yet for Katharine. Indeed, she had so prolonged her work by glooming over it, that it was quite late in the afternoon before she went up to her little room and began slowly to smooth her hair. Her mother's voice called from the sewing room where she had been all day with the dressmaker. "Katharine, Mrs. Whiting has just turned the corner, and is coming this way. She has come down very early. You will have to go downstairs and receive and entertain her for a while, until I can come. I am sorry, but I cannot possibly leave this work just now. Do the best you can, dear."

That was all; and then the door of the sewing room

shut quickly, and the hurried mother went back to
her work, while Katharine scowled harder than
ever, and went slowly, crossly, down to the door to
welcome old Mrs. Whiting. Her greeting was by no
means cordial; and her mode of entertaining her was
so stiff and disagreeable that the poor lady felt quite
ill at ease, until at last the gentle mother came down,
and Katharine was set free to attend to the supper.

"I shall not be able to go to prayer meeting tonight, daughter; I feel one of my nervous headaches
coming on, and shall have to go to bed. You can go to
the meeting with Mrs. Whiting, dear, can't you?"

This sentence, spoken at the tea table, with old
Mrs. Whiting sitting opposite to her and listening,
seemed to Katharine the climax of the ugly day. Of
course there was nothing to be said but "Yes," when
she was asked before everyone. She thought to herself as she went for her hat and jacket, "Is all the
winter to be like this, I wonder? Oh, what a contrast
to yesterday!"

Prayer meeting seemed the height of dreariness to
Katharine tonight. She was never at any time fond
of going, and usually got out of it as often as she
could. To think of having to sit in that dark little
room, where all the lamps smoked and the air
smelled strongly of kerosene, and listen to several
long prayers and talks by some old men and women!
She recoiled from the idea, and thought, as she had
done a dozen times that day, of the evening before,
and the merry party that had gathered at one of the
pleasant homes in the village for a farewell frolic.

The meeting was not quite as dreary as she had

pictured it. More were out than usual, and there was a spirit of earnestness in all that was said that would have surprised her if she had not been too much wrapped up in her morbid thoughts to pay any attention to what was going on. But the air was as full of kerosene and dust as she had expected, and she turned up her nose over it, and wished for the end of the meeting to come.

At last the day was over, and Katharine was seated in her room with the little package in her lap, and leisure to open it. She untied the strings slowly, thinking of the dear friends who had left it, wondering to herself why the summer could not have lasted longer, and why it was that a winter with its hard work must come.

I I .   D I F F E R E N C E

The package proved to be made up of several smaller ones. Each of the girls had remembered her with some little parting gift, and the several packages were characteristic of the donors. The first contained a dainty pair of kid gloves, well chosen for the one who was to wear them, and perfect in size, shape, and color. These were from Fannie, who enjoyed pretty clothes so much. Next, a small volume of essays from Mabel, the literary member of the company. From Frances, the needleworker, a small sachet bag, elaborate in satins of delicate shades and exquisitely painted bolting cloth. It looked like Frances, and the faint, sweet odor of it reminded one of her. Then from Cousin Hetty, a blank book, bound in leather, with pockets in the covers, ample pages dated for each day of the year, and a lovely fountain pen with gold-banded cap. This was to be used as a diary, and to be written in every day, so said a note slipped inside the cover. "Keep log notes, you know, Kathie, as they do on shipboard, for us to read next summer when we all come back. And you must put down your real thoughts too—your own original ones—so that we can live your winter over with you next year."

Katharine curled her lip as she finished reading this note, and her eyes were filled with that gloomy discontent which had shone so plainly all day upon her face. What was there for her to write that the girls would care to live over with her next summer? How would they stand it if they really had to live it with her, or in her place? It was easy enough for them to write pleasant things that happened, and make them interesting, too, with their lives full of boarding school and lectures and concerts, and all sorts of delightful occupations; but what was she to do? There would be nothing but dishes and ripped-up dresses and dismal prayer meetings for her to write about the whole long winter through. She sighed again as she looked at the pretty things in her lap.

But the treasures were so new and precious that she sat up to examine and enjoy them once more. The sachet bag was admired again, and finally placed in her handkerchief box, carefully guarded by her finest embroidered handkerchief. The gloves were tried on, and fitted perfectly; the volume of essays was glanced into, and found to look really quite interesting. Then came the diary to be written in; for of course she must try the new pen immediately, and the book ought to be started, even if there wasn't anything to write about. She poised the pen in the air, and drew her forehead together in a thoughtful frown, and then after a few minutes dashed ahead, and began.

"I must write my thoughts in this book, they say," she wrote. "My thoughts for every day; but I have no thoughts that are pleasant to write today. My pleasant thoughts are all of yesterday. Oh, if it were back! If I could see the girls once more! If I could live the summer over again! It was so bright and happy! Yesterday the hill looked so lovely, the tennis court was so delightful; and now all have a lonely, don't-care look. I cannot see the use in a life that is all made up of washing dishes and going to poky prayer meetings. Such a life as Mrs. Whiting has! I wonder if I shall ever care for it when I get to be an old lady. It doesn't seem as if I could stand to be an old lady, anyway. Think of having to come down here to tea, where nobody wants her, in order to get any pleasure! Oh, it is awful! I wonder why people can't stay young always. I wish I was rich! I can't understand why everyone can't be rich. It wouldn't hurt anyone! I am just tired of having only one servant—and she has to go home every day or two to take care of some sick sister or other—and ripping up old dresses. I wish I never had to wear another made-over dress. I *hate* them!"

Under this word hate she made a black, crooked little flourish, and stopped a moment with a mark just like it puckered into her forehead, and her lips twisted into the shape of the word hate. Then she seemed to realize a little what sort of a spirit she had been showing all day, and what she had put upon the clear, white sheet before her; and she bent her head once more, and wrote: "Oh, how ugly I am, anyway! I wish I could be different; but I can't."

She put the cap on her pen, and with a long-drawn sigh placed it in its little case. But in opening the cover of the book she discovered a small slip of paper. She pulled it out, wondering if it were another note from Hetty. No; it was only a little printed card. The heading caught her eye—"Difference," in large letters. It seemed a queer title for anything. She read the first line:

I was poor yesterday, but not today.

She smiled half sneeringly to herself. That wasn't her case. She might be said to have been rich yesterday, but today there was nothing but drudgery and dismal prospects. She read on, to discover why the individual who wrote it was poor no longer.

I was poor yesterday, but not today;
    For Jesus came this morning
And took the poor away;
    And he left the legacy
He promised long ago.
    So peace and joy and love
Through all my being flow.

A strange feeling took possession of her as she read the quaint little poem:

I was tired yesterday, but not today.
I could run and not be weary,
This blessed way;
For I have his strength to stay me,
With his might my feet are shod.
I can find the resting places
In the promises of God.

A servant yesterday, a child today,
A loved one of his household,
Bearing his name alway.
Do you know this blessed difference?
Do you long for this better way?
He will come to you as he came to me
With the joy of an endless day.

No, she did not know that difference, and she was not at all sure that she longed for that better way. Indeed, that way did not seem better to her, but it always seemed gloomy and forbidding.

It was the first time in her life that she had ever really taken into her consciousness the thought that there might be joy in the service of Christ for any but very old people who did not expect to live long anyway. There was a charm in the bit of rhyme that made her read it over again before she put it away. Was it really true that Jesus could take the "poor" and the "tired" away, and leave happiness? Had he promised a legacy to her? What was it? What were the promises of God, that made themselves into resting places? She was tired, and she wished she could feel that way, and stop thinking about yesterday. Somehow even that didn't look very bright now.

There was an uplifting about the thoughts written here that for the moment helped her to realize the comparative smallness of all other joys. She put it away in the pocket, and went about her preparations for the night; but serious thoughts of a different kind from any she had ever had before kept coming and going in her mind. At last the light was turned out, and she knelt beside her bed, as was her custom, for the few formal words of prayer which she had said every night since she was old enough to lisp the words. There had never been any real heart praying in them. It had been a mere form, gone through without much thought, and more from habit and a superstitious feeling that something would go wrong if she omitted it, than from any desire to ask anything from the Father in heaven.

But tonight as she knelt, a new feeling came to her. She seemed to be coming into a strange, mysterious Presence which she had never known before. She had not doubted that there was a God, or that he heard prayer; but the question had never had enough thought from her to be even raised in her mind. Now she seemed suddenly brought face to face with a new idea. Was God standing near listening when she spoke? Did he care to hear, and would he answer? What was this feeling that had come over her? Was it possible that he was speaking to her? Her heart had been so desolate and lonely all day, she began to feel the need of something outside herself to make her happy. A sudden longing came over her to have this wonderful "difference" in herself, to know what it was to have Jesus come and take the self-weariness

away, and make things bright for her. Half unbe-
lieving that there was such a thing, or that Christ
would or could give her a real joy, she followed a
sudden impulse, and resolved to tell him all about it.
"O Jesus Christ," she prayed, "I am so tired of myself! If there is any way to make me different, please
do." She was not much used to praying, except in
formal words, and so the words did not come freely;
but she knelt long, her lips not framing any words,
but her heart sending forth an earnest petition for
something to satisfy the great longing in her heart.

She relighted the lamp again before she lay down,
and took down her Bible that had been neglected
much, opening at random, and beginning to read at
the first place. It proved to be the eleventh chapter
of Matthew. She read on without much taking in the
meaning of the words, until she came to the last
three verses: "Come unto me, all ye that labour and
are heavy laden, and I will give you rest. Take my
yoke upon you, and learn of me; for I am meek and
lowly of heart: and ye shall find rest unto your souls.
For my yoke is easy, and my burden is light." Of
course the words were as familiar to her as they are
to you and me; and yet, because of their familiarity,
and because of the urgent need of her soul, they
seemed to mean more to her that night than they
ever had before.

She put away the book, thinking as she once more
turned out her light and lay down, how very tired
she was, and how much she would like to be rested.
She wondered how Jesus Christ could rest her, and
whether he would, and wished it would come soon.

Then she closed her eyes, and thought of the past summer again, and of the girls. A slight smile crossed her face at thought of Cousin Hetty. Hetty would be glad if she could have seen her reading the Bible, she was sure. Hetty was a true Christian, if there ever was one; and then Katharine sighed, and thought how impossible it would be for her to ever be as good as Hetty was, and wished again she were rich, and did not have to do things she disliked.

The October wind sighed among the half-naked branches outside the window, and the distant sound of the whistle of the midnight train could be faintly heard, as Katharine dropped off to sleep.

III. FINDING REST

The next morning after breakfast, while she stood at the kitchen door waiting for some concoction on the stove to boil, Katharine thought over this matter of rest.

She was watching old Andy, the man who sawed wood for them, and wondering how he stood his cheerless life, full of hard work. Where did the rest come in for him? She resolved to ask him. He was fond of talking to Miss Katharine; and many a long sermon he had preached to her, choosing his own text. Sometimes he began:

"Ah, Miss Katharine, an' isn't this a bright, beauty morning, to be sure! Oh, how good our God is to make us such mornings! We just ought to be praisin' him all the day long. Sometimes I feel just like gettin' right down in the dust an' ashes an' a-tellin' him what a sinner I be for not bein' thankfuller for all his goodness to me."

Katharine liked to hear him talk. There was a quaint earnestness about him which always interested her, and sometimes his thoughts were original. She turned to him as he came near where she stood, to put the armful of wood he had just finished sawing on the neat pile he was constructing near the door.

"Andy," she said, more real earnestness in her voice than she was accustomed to use when speaking to the old man, "do you know that verse about 'Come unto me, all ye that labour and are heavy laden, and I will give you rest'?"

"Oh, certain, certain, miss; that I do!" responded Andy heartily, stopping in front of her, the great armful of wood clasped tight in his worn old arms. "Many's the time, miss, when I've come, weary an' heavy laden as I was, an' foun' that rest. Oh, it's wonderful! wonderful!" and he drew one hand meditatively across his eyes, then began to lay the sticks in regular rows on the pile.

"But, Andy," said Katharine, with a puzzled expression, "you have to work hard all the time just the same. I don't see as you've been given any rest."

"Surely, Miss Katharine, you didn't suppose I was never to work again, did you? The good book never says, 'Come unto me, all ye that labor an' are heavy laden, an' I will take away your work, so that you won't have to do it any more.' Why, that would be to make a lazy set of folks of us; an' Jesus himself, when he was here on the earth, he worked hard. No; oh, no, miss! Rest never means no more work. Why, when a man's rested, he's all ready an' eager to work again, an' especially if the work's for the One who's rested him; an' I reckon all work that's right to do at all is for him. That's my way a-thinkin'. Ah, I've come to him many a time, an' he's made me all ready to go out an' go to work again. He's took the tiredness all away, an' made me new again. What would the Lord do with a lot o' laborers a-sittin' roun' on the edges o' the vineyard, a-foldin' their hands, and a-sayin', 'I'm gettin' rested'? Why, it don't take him no time at all to rest us! He can do it quick's we ask him, or quicker, too, for the matter o' that. It just 'pears to me that that there verse about restin' is the unlaziest verse in the hull Bible; 'cause if a man's got rest, what need's he of it? Course he'll go right to work."

Something was boiling over, and Katharine was obliged to go in and attend to it; and Andy went back to his saw again, humming in a quavering old voice:

Work, for the night is coming,
When man works no more.

Katharine, as she stirred the boiling mixture on the stove, told herself she needed rest; for she certainly did not feel like working at anything, and wondered how she could get it. Instantly came the answer in the words of her text: "Come unto me, and *I* will give you rest."

But there was really very little time to think about that or anything else. The day was even fuller of duties than the one before. There was much nerve-trying ripping, work that had to be done carefully, lest a little slip of knife or scissors should cut the goods. Besides, the dress she was ripping was for herself, and was one that she had never liked. To add to the disagreeableness of her task, there was no possibility of bettering the dress by having it made over in any very pleasing fashion; for everyone was wearing long, straight-up-and-down dresses, with little or no drapery, and this dress had been made with much half-length drapery, and all the breadths were hopelessly short. Katharine's temper was by no means smooth when she had finished her work and sat down to the dinner table with her father, mother, and brother.

Her brother was a little younger than herself, but tall for his age, and would easily pass for a year or two older than he was; but they were never much together. The truth was, there were many particularly trying things to Katharine about her brother. She often wondered why it was that he always had to act so shy and awkward, and almost disagreeable, whenever he went among people with her, and especially when there were summer guests in town. Besides, he smoked cigarettes—when he was out of his mother's sight—and always had the odor of the corner grocery about him. Katharine wished much that her brother were like some other girls' brothers, but never dreamed that she was in the least to blame for the sort of brother he was. Now, as she sat down to the table opposite him, with her nerves all unstrung over the utterly impossible task of planning a stylish suit out of the old brown cashmere, her eye fell upon the bright colors of her brother's new necktie, and it struck her as extremely loud and out of taste. It was a little thing, perhaps, to put one out of temper with one's brother; but the inharmony of the colors jarred her, and expressed in one flaring, tangible thought the whole idea of the difference between her brother and some other boys she knew. She fixed her eyes upon the offending bit of silk; and all the disappointment and ill-temper of the morning, and, indeed, of the day before, vented itself in some sharp words she said to John about his tie.

Now, John was good-natured, and usually replied to any sharp words of his sister in bright, funny retorts, until father and mother would break down in a laugh, and the whole would end in merriment; but today his face clouded over, and the color rose in his cheeks. The truth was, he did not like the tie much himself. He had good taste, and knew as well as his sister when a thing was becoming. But he had wanted some money very much for some scheme of his, and this tie had been a little cheaper than the one he preferred, so on a sudden impulse he had bought it.

"If you don't like my tie, you needn't look at it!" he retorted in a gruff tone. "There are plenty of other directions to look. You get so set up with all your elegant young gentlemen here in the summer, you can't speak decently to your own brother anymore. I'd just like to have that snob of a Frank Warner see you now. He'd think you were a perfect angel." And he broke off his sentence with a rough laugh.

It was Katharine's turn to flash her eyes and grow

red in the face now, and more sharp words came from her lips.

It was a very uncomfortable dinner. Of course the father checked John in the midst of his bitter reply to Katharine, and then administered a sharp rebuke to Katharine, which brought the red still deeper to her cheeks. John swallowed his dinner rapidly, declined any dessert, and then departed, while his mother looked after him with a weary, anxious face, and sighed; and the father, following her troubled glance, grew more severe of countenance, and said to Katharine, "If you would devote a little more of your time to your own brother, and less to other girls' brothers, he might turn out more to your liking."

Then Katharine left the table in a deluge of tears, and spent the rest of the afternoon in her own room, alternately blaming and pitying herself. The father and mother, left to enjoy their dinner alone, ate little, and sat for the most part in troubled silence, wondering what they had done or left undone in bringing up their children that they should turn out in such a disappointing way.

Already to Katharine the dreaded long winter seemed far on its way. It could not be, she thought, that it was only two days since the girls and boys had all been here. Oh, if the winter were ended, and a new summer begun! She thought over the scene at the dinner table. How dreadful it was to have her father talk so to her about John! What could she have done? Anything? No; John was not like others. He did not care for anything she did. If he only did, what a comfort he might be! And she fell to picturing him as she would like to have him. But her thoughts ended in her feeling quite well satisfied with her own conduct, and very much dissatisfied with her brother. Still, she was unhappy. She thought often also during the afternoon of the "rest," and wished she knew exactly how to "come" in the right way, that she might be sure to get it. Nevertheless, when she prayed that night, though she asked to be shown how to come, she asked in a halfhearted way, and not at all as if it were the one great desire of her life. She looked back to the bright days of fun and frolic as even more desirable. She wrote much in her new diary that night about longing to have rest. She carefully recalled and noted down what Andy had said about it, and thought with satisfaction of the delight with which the girls would read this entry next summer; for she knew they would appreciate and enjoy Andy's quaintness as much as she had.

As she had read over what she had written, Satan, leaning over her shoulder, whispered in her ear that it sounded very well; and I am sure that if her good angel had not put the thought into her heart to take out the little poem once more and read it over, she would have gone to bed that night with too high an estimate of herself.

I can find my resting places
In the promises of God.

These two lines of the poem kept saying themselves over after she had lain down. What were some of the promises of God? She tried to think of one. "I will give you rest." The words seemed to speak themselves to her. She had not realized that this was a promise in which she could have sure confidence. She fell asleep with a feeling that she could and would find that rest somewhere.

IV. THE ANSWER

It seemed a strange thing to Katharine that the next Sunday morning the minister should take for his text those very verses about which she had thought so much during the week. She looked up at him with startled eyes when he announced it, as though he must surely have been reading her thoughts. She had not wanted to go to church at all that morning. Indeed, she never was fond of going; and today it seemed lonely to go and miss the bright faces of her various friends. She had tried to think up a good excuse, but none was forthcoming, and so she went. She was not in the habit of giving much heed to the sermon, but this morning her attention was caught and fixed before she was aware of it; indeed, she scarcely took her eyes from the minister's face until he had finished.

He spoke forcibly and clearly about the way to "come"; dwelt for a few moments on the wonderful rest that God could give; but the main part of his sermon was about the thoughts in the last verse, "Take my yoke upon you, and learn of me." He made it appear that it was the duty of everyone who had come to Christ to take his yoke. Then he told how a yoke was something to make work easier, and that

Christ's putting this sentence right after the other one about coming to him, showed that he wanted and expected everyone who came to him to go to work immediately. Some yokes were made for two, he said, with one end heavier than the other. Christ's yoke was like this and he would work with us and bear the heavy end of the yoke, so that our work might not be too great for our strength. That work could not help but be easy and beautiful with Jesus Christ to help and to go with us, wearing the same yoke. He closed with the words, "For my yoke is easy, and my burden is light." And Katharine felt that she had never known what those words meant before.

It was a simple sermon, perhaps might have been called commonplace by some; but either Katharine's eyes were getting opened to see new things in the words of truth, or else she had never listened before, for she thought it a wonderful sermon. She looked about on the congregation when it was finished, and felt surprised to find Deacon Ewing yawning, and Mrs. Moffat evidently awaking from a refreshing nap, while her brother John's eyes were just returning from a trip over the ceiling.

John Bowman did not often go to church. This had been one of the mornings when he did not exactly know what to do with himself, and, not enjoying his own company well enough to stay at home without something interesting to read, had gone, just because he did not know what else to do. He had not listened to the sermon. Not he. He had thought of a thousand different schemes for employing that hour since he had been in church, and he wished with all his heart that he had stayed at home and carried some of them out. He resolved that it would be some time before he came again.

Katharine, wondering whether she had a work, and how she could begin to put on that yoke, glanced at her brother and in some way connected him with the sermon. She remembered her father's sentence at the dinner table some days before, "If you would devote a little more time to your brother, he might turn out more to your liking," and, sighing, wished she could do something in that direction. She watched him not a little during the closing hymn, and tried to think up some way of helping him. Nothing occurred to her except the evening service. She remembered having heard among the announcements of a young people's prayer meeting. She had a vague idea that it was by prayer meetings and churchgoing that people were made different; and perhaps John would get some good from attending. Anyway, it would keep him from going off with some of the boys who were doing him no good. She decided, therefore, to try to get him to go that evening. To be sure, she had never been to the young people's meeting herself, and had an idea that it was a very dull affair; but the whole service that morning had been so in harmony with the little poem she was growing fond of, that she was seized with a longing to go herself, and see if she could get some help. Having made the resolve to try and do something for John, she felt very meritorious; but when the afternoon came, and the evening drew on, and she met

John in the hall on his way to his room, she found it was easier to resolve than to put into practice. Somehow, it was a very awkward thing for this sister to ask her brother to accompany her to prayer meeting. It was strange that all the cross, sharp words which she had ever spoken to him seemed to troop up and stand around now to listen. Perhaps it was their mocking, scornful presence that made Katharine's voice sound unnatural and her face take on a severe cast, as she finally mustered up courage and said, "John, I wish you would go down to the young people's meeting with me tonight."

John stopped short on the top stair, turned around, looked down on her, and drew a long whistle. "The dickens, you do!" said he in a surprised tone; then as he caught the severity of her face his own grew dark, his voice changed, and he said in quite a different tone, "How long since you've had to take up with your brother's company? You must be hard up if you can't scratch around and find someone else. Not much I won't! To prayer meeting? The idea! I didn't know you were fond of that sort of thing yourself." He gave a scornful laugh, and went to his room.

Of course it made Katharine very angry to have what she considered sisterly advances treated in this way, and she made up her mind never to try again. She went to her room in a fit of what she thought was righteous indignation, and treated her brother with a frigid dignity at the tea table. At the close of the meal, as he left the table, he said to her in an offhand way, "I'm goin' down past the church, Kate;

and if you want to go to that meeting, you can come along with me. There'll be plenty of folks for you to come home with. The Moffats always go, you know."

It was quite a condescension for John to say this; but Katharine was too much on her dignity to accept it. She spoke coldly, "Thank you; I can get there in the same way, then, if I care to go, without troubling you."

"All right!" John said, with a careless shrug of his shoulders, as he went out of the room.

Katharine did not go to the meeting that night. Instead, she shut herself into her room, and began thinking. She was very unhappy. At first the unhappiness vented itself in anger toward her brother, and a self-righteous feeling that she had done her duty; but this did not satisfy her. There seemed an emptiness about everything in which she tried to interest herself. She read the little poem over line by line, and tried to imagine herself saying it truly from her heart.

So peace and joy and love
Through all my being flow.

Why, peace was calm and deep and restful; and joy was uplifting; and love—why, love was the best, the sweetest, the greatest, the happiest thing in all the world! What would it be like to have them flow through all her being?

Do you know this blessed difference?
  Do you long for this better way?
He will come to you as he came to me,
  With the joy of an endless day.

Yes, she did long for this better way with all her heart. Oh, would he come to her? She bowed her head in her hands, and burst into tears, wondering why she felt so miserable. She had never felt so before. She had never known these intense longings for something better, and could not understand it now. She did not know that at that very moment, away in a western city, Cousin Hetty knelt in prayer, pouring out her heart to God for her with an earnestness and faith that would not be denied. Neither could she know that in one of the rooms of an eastern college a young man also knelt and prayed for her. Such earnest, united prayers could not fail to bring an answer. Katharine would have been surprised to know that Frank Warner was praying for her; for although she knew he was one of the divinity students, and expected to become a minister, yet he had never said or done anything to make her think he took a special interest in her personal salvation or that of anyone else. But since Frank had returned to college he had met with some earnest souls who had put new life into his own heart, and his conscience began to reproach him for the long summer spent in idleness in the Lord's vineyard. As he grew nearer to the Master he began to have a great longing for his friends to come; and he thought of the bright girl who had been the life of their little company all summer, and wished that she, too, might find the Savior.

If Katharine had known all this, it might have hastened her decision. While she sat in her room, desolate and perplexed, her mind went back to the morning sermon, and a few sentences of it came clearly before her: "Christ says, 'Come unto me.' The first duty of a sinner is to *come*. One must not seek to appease an offended God by doing good works. Your works are not accepted by him until you have obeyed him and 'come.' How shall you come? Kneel down before him. Tell him you are wretched and sorrowful; that you need him to save you; that you wish to give up all sin, and belong to him." "How simple that is!" Katharine said to herself. "Why should I not do what he has told me to? If he wants me to come, why should I not? I will."

God's promise is sure. When Katharine arose from her knees she was surprised to discover what a new feeling of peace had come into her heart. She went to her window, and looked out upon the clear, starlit October sky. The bright lights shining there so steadily and kindly seemed to look down on her like the eye of God; and there came to her a sudden realization that now she could repeat the poem, and feel that she meant every word of it.

I was tired yesterday, but not today.
I could run and not be weary,
This blessed way;
For I have his strength to stay me,
With his might my feet are shod.
I can find my resting places
In the promises of God.

She turned from the window with a joy in her heart that had never been there before.

V . A WORK TO DO

While Katharine was getting breakfast Monday morning, old Andy came in with wood to fill the box behind the stove. He dusted his hands off, after laying the wood nicely in the box, and stood a moment with his rough fingers spread out before the fire. It was a chilly morning, and the warmth was grateful to those worn, hard-worked hands.

"Oh, an' wasn't that a sermon, Miss Katharine?" he said, as he moved his hands to let the warmth reach every part of them. "It jus' did my heart good. It jus' do seem that the preacher have the truth hid in his heart, an' he know how to tell it out too! An' that is a wonderful text, that is. I've been a-thinkin' about it greatly since you spoke of it last week. I have been a-thinkin' how we jus' ought to get right down on our knees an' thank the Lord every day that he be so kind an' willin' as to let us take his yoke upon us, an' that he will bear it with us. Instead o' that, we some of us go on every day, an' never so much as try to get the yoke to make the work easy. Why, Miss Katharine, I've many a time laid out to do a piece of work which I thought would benefit the Lord a great deal. I jus' went ahead and tried it, an' 'twouldn't work—o' course 'twouldn't. People, when they doos those things without consultin' the Lord to see if it's what he would have 'em do, has jus' got to make up their minds that 'twon't work. They ain't a-wearin' his yoke when they go on that line. Why, you see the verse goes on to say, 'And learn of me,' an' if they ain't a-learnin' of him they ain't got on his yoke, that's all. There's a heap of work a-lyin' round, ready cut out an' basted, fur us to go at; an' if we prefer to go ahead an' cut out our own work, without even asking him fer his pattern and gettin' his advice, we kin decide it'll be a failure an' a botch; that's the whole story. That's what my mother used to tell the girls when they wanted to make their own dresses 'fore they was old enough an' wise enough; an' they tried it once or twice, an' they see 'twas jus' as she said. It don't pay to go to work 'thout learnin' of him." And the old man shook his head thought-fully, and looked at the glowing coals.

"How can you learn of him, Andy?" asked Katharine. She was interested in this subject. It struck home. She thought of her own small attempt at work yesterday, and its failure, and wondered if here were not the secret of her difficulty.

"Learn o' him? Why, jus' go an' get acquainted with him. You want to read the Book about him, an' get so well acquainted with him as he was, that you know jus' what he'd do if he was in your place. Then you have to ask him to help, you know; an' he always do that. He allus carry the heavy end of the yoke hisself."

"But it would take a long time to find out all about him," said Katharine, "and Mr. Richards said that people ought to go right to work as quick as they belong to him. One would have to read the Bible through to know all about him, and then they couldn't remember half they read."

"Oh, but, Miss Katharine, you do not need to wait. You go to our Father, an' he takes you, an' you ask him to put you to work, an' he says, 'I will, my child';

an' you ask him to take your wicked, sinful heart away, an' give you a good heart, an' he puts his Spirit in your heart, an' then you keep your eyes wide open, an' begin to learn about him, an' love him as fas' as you can, an' begin to love everybody else, an' you'll see plenty to do fer 'em. You grow so you find the work popping up at every turn. You may set it down as pretty sure that when you find a place you can't work in, or when you do something where you can't see a bit of work to do for him, then you better get out of it. It ain't the vineyard if there ain't any work in it for you, an' his children has no business anywhere outside of the vineyard fer a minit."

"But," said Katharine, half-laughing at the odd way in which he put it, "that can't be true, Andy, for that would cut a Christian off from ever playing any games, or having any good times."

"How so, Miss Katharine? I can't see 'twould work that way."

"Why, Andy, people can't do any good by playing games. There is no possible way in which they could do any work for the Lord that way."

"Better stop it, then, Miss Katharine. But I don't see it that way. There's that there pretty game you play out on my green lawn that I mowed so nice for you the other day, where you have a fishnet, strung up, and knock little white balls over it. I can't play it myself, but I like to see it, an' I feel every time when I see some of you young folks out there playin', an' a-seemin' to enjoy it all so much, that that's just what our Father wants us to do. I can think o' lots o' ways that there game might be made to come inside the vineyard. There ain't nothin' at all to prevent. I s'pose you could find a whole lot in this very town that would give their two eyes to get a chance at that there bat an' ball, an' be allowed to skip 'round on that pretty grass. Then you know we were told to go fishin' after other folks, an' bring 'em into the kingdom; an' it 'pears to me that there game would make jus' the best kind of bait. You young folks all seem to enjoy it so much, that it stands to reason other young folks would too; an' if they could be given a chance, perhaps 'twould give you a hold on 'em, an' then the way o' the Lord would open wide enough, an' you would find the harvest in your corner o' the vineyard bigger than you could tend to all by yourself, an' you'd have to call in someone to help you. But I must be a-goin' now; I've got warm. You jus' try that game, Miss Katharine, an' see ef it don't make good bait. Good-mornin'."

Katharine was astonished over this part of the conversation. It had not occurred to her as possible that she could work by means of her pleasures. She had sorrowfully packed her rackets away in flannel only a day or two before, thinking that she should have no more tennis until the next summer. Hers was the only tennis court in the village, and she was the only one of the young people living there who played or understood the game at all. Now a new thought had come to her. Perhaps she might make her tennis help. She was very quiet at the breakfast table, thinking about it, but coming to no conclusion until she heard her brother say, "It's dreadfully boring nowadays. I wish there was a circus or a county fair or a baseball game to see, or something going on"; and he yawned and scowled, and looked out of the window in a hopelessly dreary way.

A thought came to Katharine. She waited a minute, considering it before she spoke, and then said, "John, suppose you come up this afternoon about half-past three, and play tennis with me."

It was said in a pleasant tone, and there was actually a smile on Katharine's face. John looked at her with amazement a moment, and then decided to take it all as a joke, and replied in a gruff tone, "I can't play tennis."

"Well, it's very easy to learn. I think I can teach you in a little while so that you can beat me. Boys always play better than girls after they get a start," said Katharine pleasantly.

"Do you mean it, really?" said John, looking pleased, and beginning to take an interest. "I always thought I'd like to play, but never could get a chance to get the hang of the thing when there wasn't anyone around watching. I didn't want to make a fool of myself, and none of 'em seemed to want me, anyway; so I kept out of the way."

It was strange what an effect this had upon Katharine. She felt ashamed and glad and sorry, all in one. To think that her brother had wanted to join in her pleasure, and had been kept out partly by herself! Perhaps he might have been as good a player as anyone, and have learned many things from associations with the others. She was gleeful, too, to think that the "bait," as Andy had called it, had taken so well at the start. She resolved to do her best toward making her brother John love tennis as well as she did.

"But I haven't any racket," said John, a dismayed look coming over his face, as he suddenly thought of a new objection. But then he smiled.

"Oh, yes! there's one. Cousin Hetty left hers. She said it wasn't of any use to take it home, because she wouldn't be where she could play all the fall, and she expected to be back here early in the spring. She said I could use it whenever I wanted to."

Katharine went about her work after breakfast with a lighter heart than she had carried since her friends left. There was something very pleasant in anticipating a game of tennis, considering that she had not played for nearly a week, and that she had supposed that pleasure over for the summer. Then it was interesting to try to teach her brother. But beneath it all was a joy which she had scarcely begun to understand yet—the joy of doing work for Christ.

VI. THE BAIT

The game of tennis was quite successful. John proved an apt scholar, and before long could hit the ball in a very commendable manner. Then, too, he gained a new respect for his sister when he found she could strike and place a ball so that he could not reach it. He made up his mind to become a good player, and be equal with her. So he put his will to it, and straightway won a game from her. They played on till called to tea, and then came in with bright eyes and glowing cheeks, laughing and talking together as their mother had not seen them do since they were little children. Katharine felt proud of John, and told with glee some comical remark of his to her father and mother at the supper table. Her father looked at her in a pleased way, and the mother dropped her anxious, worried expression. Altogether it was a very happy evening. John stayed at home, and Katharine spent some time in explaining to him the intricacies of a game with four players; and they decided that after he had had a little more practice they would try to get some of the other young people in town to purchase rackets and learn the game, so that they might have a full set. Really, John was growing almost as enthusiastic over it as Katharine. It was quite a new order of things for him to take such interest in home amusements, and it made his mother's troubled heart glad.

It became the rule now to play tennis every afternoon; and soon two other young people came to learn. The autumn was stretched out much beyond its usual length; and many days that were, strictly speaking, early winter, were warm enough to be delightful for tennis. There was no mistaking the fact that tennis had taken a firm hold on John Bowman, and was rapidly growing popular with several other young people in the village. Katharine, who had always been so reserved, and had kept much to herself when her summer friends were not with her, was becoming the center of attraction. She was rather astonished when she realized it herself, and remembered Andy's words, "I think that there game would make good bait." It was very evident that the bait was good, but she began to question whether she were using it in the right way. She had gone for several weeks to the young people's prayer meeting, and was becoming quite interested in it. She had even timidly ventured to recite a Bible verse once or twice; but she had never invited John since that first night in which he had repulsed her. Now she began to think about the matter again. He had not been to church since that Sunday when the sermon had so impressed her. She was much troubled about him. She was beginning to love him in a different, more interested way than she had ever loved him before. Indeed, she had been praying for him not a little lately, but in that timid, half-unbelieving way in which we sometimes pray for our friends, feeling that God has told us to do it. We wish them to be different, but we cannot see how it is possible that they can be changed. The wished-for alteration may come in the distant future, but in some mysterious, gradual way. Therefore, we feel no need for undue haste or earnestness.

Katharine had been thinking it over one morning, and had resolved that she would make another attempt to get John to the young people's meeting. She had just decided how she would introduce the subject, and was smiling over the way in which she thought her brother would reply, when she heard a ring at the doorbell, and went to answer it.

It was a young lady, a little older than Katharine, a member of the young people's society. She had come to see if Katharine would lead the next Sunday evening's meeting. She asked it in a quiet, matter-of-fact tone, as if she supposed, of course, it would be the most natural thing in the world for Katharine to say "Yes." But Katharine's heart came up and stood in her mouth in amazement and horror. She lead a meeting? No, indeed! She could not possibly do it! She was sorry they had thought of such a thing. She never could lead a meeting; she would break down.

Then the young woman looked at her kindly, and said, "Dear Miss Bowman, do you think it is right for a child of the heavenly Father to feel that way?"

"Right?" said Katharine in amazement.

"Yes, right. You have no physical inability. You are perfectly able to conduct the meeting. You help us in everything else. In all our socials and concerts and entertainments you are willing to take prominent parts. Why should you be unwilling, then, to lead the meeting? We all take our turn; why should you not do it too? You surely are not ashamed of your Savior?"

"No," said Katharine, with burning cheeks and eyes cast down; "but I'm sure I never could do that. I'm not good enough. Why, I've only just begun myself!"

"We do not any of us feel that we have much goodness, Miss Bowman; and I think you will find that even if you have just started out, this will be a help to you. It was to me. I felt stronger after I had done something like this. It is witnessing for him, you know. And really I think you exaggerate the duties of a leader. It is nothing so very difficult that you have to do. We usually open with singing once or twice, and then prayer and the reading of the Bible. The topic is selected on our cards, you know; and you can say a few words about the verses, or not, as you like. After that there are usually several short prayers. Why, the meeting will run itself; it only needs a head. But we want you very much to join in with us and help. Can't you do it for Christ's sake? He has done so much for us, you know; it seems a small thing for us to do for him."

But it required much more persuasion and argument before Katharine, with almost trembling lips, and eyes that were brimful of tears, murmured a low, "I will try."

Her heart trembled many times for the next few days over what she had promised to do, and she wished again and again that she could take back her promise. She spent many hours over her Bible, studying what she should say; but she did not carry out her plan for inviting her brother to attend the meeting. That was more than flesh and blood could stand, she thought, to lead a meeting, and have one's brother there besides.

Sunday morning came at last, and Katharine compromised with her conscience by asking John to go to church in the morning. He surely ought to do that; and it was not to be expected that it would be possible to get him to go twice in one day. John went to church, and really seemed to listen part of the time. Katharine spent the whole afternoon in her room with her Bible, and much of the time she was upon her knees asking God's Spirit to help her. She seemed to come nearer to her heavenly Father that afternoon than ever before, and to feel his hand upon her, and to hear his voice saying, "Be not afraid, neither be thou dismayed; for the Lord thy God is with thee whithersoever thou goest."

When she came downstairs, ready for meeting, there was a more peaceful expression on her face, and her heart felt a little more assured over the new duty which she was going out to perform.

But her brother John met her in the hall below. "Where are you going, Kathie?" he asked. "To that meeting? Guess I'll go with you, and see what it's like."

The Katharine of other days might have told him coldly that she did not wish his company, or preferred to go alone, or something of that sort; but she did not dare to do so now, after wishing so long that he would go.

They walked out the door and down the street in silence, the sister's heart throbbing painfully. How could she lead that meeting with her brother there? All her past inconsistencies and disagreeableness arose before her, and threatened to kill her with the awful weight of their immensity. She bowed her head in the darkness, and tried to press back the tears that were on the verge of rolling down her cheeks. At last she made a desperate effort at self-control, and said in rapid, trembling voice, "John, perhaps you won't like it if I don't tell you beforehand. *I'm* going to lead that meeting tonight."

It was out now; and she shuddered to think how hard it had been, and hoped with her whole heart that John would say that he guessed he had better not go, that it might be embarrassing, or something of the sort. But no; he only drew a long whistle, and said, "The dickens, you are! Well, I'm glad I picked out tonight to sample it, then. I didn't know you ever did that sort of thing."

"I never did before, John. I don't know how I shall get on. But I am trying to please Christ now. I am almost afraid to have you go, because you will think I am not in earnest about it. I am afraid you will remember how many times I have been cross and ugly to you."

The tears had actually come now, and her voice was trembling.

"Why, Kathie," said her brother, almost tenderly, touched and embarrassed, and scarcely knowing what to say to this unusual outburst, "you're just splendid now! You don't get cross anymore—much. I wondered what it was about. But you can lead a meeting better than the whole lot of 'em put together, I'll bet. Don't you worry."

V I I .   A   N E W   L A W

Her brother's words, spoken in that new tone of disguised tenderness, helped Katharine wonderfully. She went up to the leader's seat by the little table with a feeling that she had one friend in the room at least. It was new to look to her brother for anything, and the last thing that was to be expected from him was encouragement. Could it be possible that he had learned this from her own helpful encouragement of him when he made a blunder in tennis? Katharine did not think of this as she took her seat and opened the hymnbook; she only knew that it was very pleasant to have her brother speak that way to her, and she felt a longing to have this meeting such as would help him to find Christ.

In the few words that she spoke when she bowed her head to open the meeting with prayer, she tried to forget that there was any one else present but herself and God, and she asked him to bless the meeting. The meeting did run itself, as the young committee-woman had told Katharine, and was a very earnest one. For her own part in it Katharine read the little poem which had grown so dear to her. She read it beautifully, putting her whole heart into it; and her brother, as he listened carefully to every word, noting with pride the distinct pronunciation and perfect expression, said to himself, "She means that. She feels every speck of it. She is different. I wonder what it all is, anyway." Then there came into his heart just the faintest little bit of a desire to know the wonderful difference himself.

When the meeting was over, John waited quietly for her at the door. He reached his hand for her Bible, and walked beside her without speaking for some time, but with an air of quiet respect, and an elder brotherly care of her which was quite new and pleasant. She could not speak first, her heart seemed so full. During the meeting a strange, earnest longing had come over her for him. She wanted so much to have him know the love of Christ.

"That was a first-class meeting, Katharine," he

said at last, breaking the silence with an almost embarrassed tone. "None of them can go ahead of you on leading, *I* know. You can do most anything you try, anyway."

Then the longings of the sister's heart arose to her lips: "O John," she said, her voice trembling with earnestness, "I don't know how to lead meetings, nor do any of these things. They are all new work to me; but I mean to learn, and I do wish so much you would help me!"

It was John's turn to be surprised now. He almost stopped short on the sidewalk with astonishment. "Me help!" he exclaimed. "What on earth could I do? I'm not worth much. You've told me so yourself hundreds of times."

"Oh, I know it, John!" she said in a pained voice, the tears coming quickly to her eyes, "and I'm *so* sorry. It wasn't true, and you could help me more than any other person."

"How in the world can I help you? What is it you want me to do?" asked John, quite tenderly and anxiously. He was not used to being asked by his sister for help, nor to seeing her in such a mood.

"Help me by trying to be a Christian with me. Won't you?" she asked eagerly. "We could work together, and help each other then; and I do so want you to belong to Jesus. Will you, John?" She put her hand lovingly into her brother's, and waited for his answer.

He closed his fingers about her hand with a warm, earnest pressure, and there was a manly expression on his face. He was very much touched. Perhaps his heart was all ready for the invitation, only no one had ever before given it. "What would I have to do?" he said at length, hesitatingly. Katharine had waited for his reply with her heart throbbing, and sending up eager, longing prayers to her Father in heaven to send his Spirit to speak to this dear brother.

"I am afraid I do not know very well how to tell you," she said, clasping his hand a little tighter in token of her great joy that his answer had not been "No." "I've only just begun myself, you know. The first thing is to give yourself to Jesus Christ. Tell him you want to be forgiven for all the wrong you have done, and you will be his forever, and try to please him always. Then after that pray every day for help, and read the Bible, and try harder all the time to please him. I'm only just finding out myself how to do it, and I want you to help, you know. You won't say no, will you? Oh, I need you so much!"

John hesitated, started to speak two or three times, then waited, and Katharine made several earnest pleas, always ending with her petition, "O John, won't you do it?"

At last, just as they reached their own gate, he said in a low voice, so low it was almost a whisper, "I guess so. I'll try."

"O John, I'm so glad!" she said joyfully; and she reached up to her tall young brother and kissed him. He bore the kiss with much embarrassment, and yet was pleased that she should give it. Katharine had never shown him much that she loved him, and he felt very tenderly toward her tonight. It was pleasant to have his sister care whether he became a

Christian or not, pleasant to have her want his help.
They went in the house together quietly then; and
the father and mother noticed the expression on
their faces with wonder as they entered the room.

After that the brother and sister began to get acquainted with one another as they had never done
before. They had many talks together about this new
subject which was beginning to interest them. John
was very shy whenever Katharine spoke about it,
and yet he seemed pleased. He entered into the
agreement with her at first more from a desire to
please her; but little by little he grew to understand
how much the promise he had made meant. Katharine watched over him constantly, guarding him
from temptations as often as she could. She became
wonderfully entertaining, so much so, that John began to prefer to stay at home, instead of wandering
off with "the fellows." Gradually their religious talks
grew longer, until it came about that every Sunday
afternoon, as a matter of course, John drew up a
large armchair in the library bay window, and
settled himself on the sofa opposite, motioning
Katharine to take the chair. Then the two would
read and talk together. They were trying to study
the Bible in such a way as would give them practical
help in their daily living, but did not always know
the best way to do it.

Thus the autumn slipped into the winter almost
without their knowledge, and they grew daily more
attached to one another, and more bound together
in all their duties and enjoyments. Helping each
other, they helped themselves.

Christmas came, and with it many beautiful re-
membrances from the summer friends. Katharine
opened them in surprise, and almost sighed as she
opened one small, thin package, neatly wrapped in
white paper, and addressed in a bold, clear hand.
Then she gave her undivided attention to the package, and to the letter accompanying it. The opened
paper disclosed a small white-clad book with gold
letters. *The Greatest Thing in the World* was the
title. On the flyleaf was written, "A Merry Christmas and Joyful New Year, from your friend, Frank
Warner." Katharine's cheeks flushed and a pleased
look came into her eyes as she turned to the letter.
It read:

My dear Friend,
The accompanying little book has helped me very
much, and I pass it on to you in the hope that you
will enjoy it as much as I have. It is Professor
Drummond's address on that wonderful love
chapter, 1 Cor. 13. You will notice that he asks all
who will to read that chapter every day for three
months. I have begun to do so. Will you join me in
it for the first three months of the new year? And
may the greatest, the best thing in all the world be
yours, is the wish of your friend,

Frank Warner

The next Sunday afternoon the new book was
brought out and read; and not only the sister, but the
brother, joined the young man in reading that marvelous chapter every day. It opened up to them new
thoughts. Assisted by Professor Drummond's clear,

helpful words, they studied Paul's analysis of "love," and tried to measure their own lives by it, and alter them so that they would fit the perfect pattern.

VIII. TOMORROW

It was a lovely spring day. The air was soft and caressing; the tender young leaves, which but the week before had first revealed their yellow-green edges, were dancing merrily, trying to shake the wrinkles out of their new spring dresses. The grass was made over new for the year, and was spangled with great bending daisies and saucy, nodding buttercups; and the clear blue sky looked down with just as pleased and surprised an air as it had used for all the other bright spring days of all the centuries gone before.

About the little village station the greenness and springiness crept, even up to its very door. Down the track a few yards the great black drinking hose which the engines used stood grinning, now and then sending a large, bright drop down with a gleeful splash, which bounded into little sprinkles over the board below. The bright steel rails gleamed in the sunshine, and hummed a cheerful prelude for the train that was approaching.

Katharine and her brother came with rapid steps down the street to the station. There was an eager, expectant look on Katharine's face that betokened some unusual pleasure. The house they had just left betokened it too. The windows were open, the summer curtains airing their freshness in the breeze.

Little vases of spring blossoms stood around on tiny stands; and everything seemed in summer holiday attire. And the curtains, as they blew; the rooms, in their quiet uncluttedness; the flowers—all seemed to say joyfully, "Cousin Hetty and the rest are coming today, and we are ready and glad."

All but John. He had been dreading the summer. Katharine was beginning to be "so nice"; and now, of course, all their good times would be broken up. She would go off with the rest, and he would be left to himself. He did not blame her; but he sighed a little, and looked glum over the prospect. He had objected decidedly to accompanying Katharine to the station.

"They don't know me much, and won't want to see me; and I shall feel like a cat in a strange garret," he had said.

But Katharine had drawn her arm through his, and, looking up lovingly into his face, had answered, "I intend they shall know you 'much,' and if they care to see much of me, they would better want to see you too; for they will soon find out that I can't get along without my brother."

Of course John went after that, though he did not in the least wish to; but he thought if Katharine wanted him so much he might as well gratify her.

The train proved to be seven minutes late; and as they stood on the platform waiting, Katharine looked off at the purple hills, which seemed to have planted themselves at the end of the track, and thought of that other day when she had looked gloomily forward at the winter, just passed. How bright it seemed to her now! What a difference there was in her life! It was no longer made up of much dull work, with only the little play spell of summer thrown in at long intervals, but was bright and happy all the way through. The coming of her summer friends she looked at in a different light now. It was indeed a delight to think of seeing and being with them once more; but it was, after all, but a pleasant incident, and not at all the one end and aim of existence, as heretofore. She looked at her brother proudly, comparing him with what he used to be, and wondering if the rest of the young people would see and appreciate him as she did herself. But the shriek of the whistle interrupted her meditations.

After that there was a merry bustle, a thumping of trunks, a babel of happy voices, and general confusion. John took the checks, and kept himself usefully in the background; but his sister brought him proudly forward as soon as possible. All the way home Katharine surprised the travelers by constantly appealing to John on questions connected with church work.

"I didn't know there was so much in John Bowman," said one of the girls in an undertone to her companion.

"I think he must have changed a good deal," was the murmured reply.

Notwithstanding, this same young woman was disappointed that afternoon when the girls, being eager for a first game of tennis, begged Katharine to bring her racket and help make up the set, and she replied, "I shall be busy for a little while this afternoon, but John will take my place."

There was nothing to be done but gracefully accept the situation and begin the game. She felt sure John Bowman could not play, and did not enjoy the prospect of being his partner. She changed her mind, however, before an hour had passed, and voted him a "splendid player, really quite scientific, besides being very pleasant company." Gradually they all came to accept him and enjoy him just as Katharine had intended they should.

But over his sister they were much puzzled. The Katharine of last summer was not wont to be occupied with anything that took her from their company, unless earnestly solicited by her mother to come and help her. This Katharine was busy from morning till night, and happy through it all. When she was with them, she was, as always, the life of the company; but she went from them to some duty with a complacent face, as though she really liked to go. Then she not only attended and enjoyed the prayer meetings of the church, but seemed to expect them to do so also.

When the little, leather-bound diary was brought out and read, the girls found the records very different from those they had expected. There were, indeed, many bright and original sentences, and there were whole pages of descriptions—beautiful, tender, witty, and unusual. There was a something left out, however, especially in the later entries, which had given the former Katharine's speeches much fascination, but could hardly be called quite charitable. Katharine was learning the old law of love, and putting it into practice. There were so many sympathetic, thoughtful touches in the small book, that they filled the place of the sharp sarcasms which were not present.

Cousin Hetty smiled to herself as she watched Katharine, filled almost with wonder to see how the soul in her had grown.

"She is indeed a child of the King," she wrote to her mother; "she shows it in every word and action, and John is not far behind her. Not that she is so very 'good,' as people say, or that she has attained to any perfection, but she seems to recognize Jesus Christ as the Leader of her life, the One first to be pleased always."

The young men noticed it too, when they came, and one of them felt that a prayer of his had been answered. Indeed, Frank Warner felt, as he watched Katharine day by day, that she had gone far beyond him in her Christian life.

"Miss Katharine, you seem different this summer from last," he said to her one evening as they walked down the moonlit village street, the last of the procession of young people who had gone out to enjoy the full moon. "Will you tell me how it is?"

"Am I different?" she asked, with a happy little laugh; then, more soberly, "I'm glad you think so. There ought to be a great difference, but there isn't as much as I wish."

"And what has made this difference? May I know about it?" he asked.

She was still for a moment, and then slowly, almost timidly, began to recite the little poem which had grown to seem a part of her life.

I was poor yesterday, but not today;
For Jesus came this morning,
And took the poor away.

Through to the end she repeated it, her voice very sweet and low; and he listened, taking the words into his heart, to be kept for a sacred memory.

"That is the reason why there is a difference," she said, "if there is any. The restlessness and uneasiness are all gone from my heart now. I feel as if Jesus had forgiven me. Your little book has helped me too. I have read that chapter of Corinthians every day this year, and it grows more wonderful every time I read it."

The moonlight sifting through the leaves made a corridor of soft light for them to walk in. The hum of the crickets, the occasional lifting of some leaf by the night wind, and worried song of a mother bird singing a late lullaby to her babies—all seemed to lend a solemn quiet to the air about, and to help them to talk about this great subject, and open their hearts to one another as they had not done before. Gradually the voices of the others grew fainter, as the steps of these two grew slower, and they held sweet conversation about their heavenly Father. It seemed, indeed, as though he were near, listening; and when, in the quietness of her own room that night, Katharine thought over that walk and talk, the words of a familiar old poem came to her mind.

And the Lord, standing quietly by
  In the shadows dim,
Smiling, perhaps, in the darkness,
  To hear our sweet, sweet talk of him.

There came a day, at the close of the summer, when Katharine stood beside the front gate once more, thinking. The summer friends had all flitted again, and another winter was about to begin; but Katharine was not dreaming of her yesterday this time, nor even of her today, but was taking a little peep into a very bright tomorrow—a tomorrow in which she was to help Frank Warner be a good minister, and he was to help her be the minister's wife.

John came down the walk and stood beside her, resting his hand upon her shoulder. She looked up at his face, and saw in it a little of that sense of left-aloneness which had made her so miserable a year ago, and she roused from her sweet thoughts to cheer him up.

But John will never be troubled by the dreariness of a today; for his sister no longer lives in her yester-days, and he has learned the secret of marking all the todays bright by looking forward to a joyful to-morrow.

AN EXCUSE
FOR CHRIST

*I*T was Wednesday evening, and the minister's family had just returned from prayer meeting. The minister threw himself wearily into one of his low study chairs, and shaded his face with his hand. The bright moonlight streamed through the window by his side, and made a soft pathway over the carpet at his feet, but he did not notice it. Through the open door another pathway of light from the hall lamp almost met the moonlight. The minister's wife stood in this pathway, and threw a long shadow across the room. She was slowly pulling off her gloves, and casting uneasy glances at the dim outline of her husband. Lily, her young sister, who was there on a visit, stood in the hall by the hat rack, taking off her hat, and pushing up the fluffy hair on her forehead.

Presently Mr. Murray broke the silence. "We might as well give up the prayer meeting. The people won't come."

"Why, James!" exclaimed his astonished wife. "Give up the prayer meeting! You surely don't mean that!"

"I do mean it. Just look at it, Mattie. Here it was a lovely night, the church was brightly lit, everything was favorable to a good attendance. And who was there? Old Deacon Eldred and his wife, who are hardly able to come out, and Mrs. Moker, who is too deaf to hear a word that's said, and Father Fisk, who always makes the same prayer, and the two Brunig sisters, and no one but yourself and Lily who could sing at all. It's a mere farce calling it a church prayer meeting. There are two hundred and fifty-seven members of this church, and there weren't but seven out to meeting. It would be a great deal better to invite them to our house than to have them rattling around in the four corners of that large room." Here the minister smiled a sad, faint smile, and leaned back again in his chair.

"It's a perfect shame!" said his wife, as she untied her bonnet strings.

"I'm sure I've tried to make the meetings interesting," came from behind the minister's hand; "but Deacon Eldred always goes to sleep—he's getting old, you know—and Father Fisk doesn't understand anything but the very simplest sentences. If only more would come!"

"Never mind," said Mrs. Murray. "We haven't been here very long, and you know they told you the people were not in the habit of attending the prayer meeting regularly. Perhaps they will do better after a while. Why, we haven't been here but eight weeks!

You make the meetings so interesting that they can't help but come soon, I'm sure."

"My dear!" said Mr. Murray, in a tone bordering just the least bit on the impatient, "how can they know that the meetings are interesting when they don't come near them to find out? I can't understand how people who are under covenant vows to attend the regular services of the church can have so far forgotten their vows as to habitually stay away from prayer meeting."

Lily turned away from the glass with a last brush of the hair, and went to the doorway. "They ought to have such an article in their church creed as we have in the constitution of our young people's society of Christian Endeavor at home," said she.

"What is that?" asked Mrs. Murray in a rather abstracted tone.

"Why, they are required to send a written excuse when they are absent from the regular monthly consecration meeting, and it must be an excuse that they can conscientiously give to God. The excuses are read in the meetings, and it adds a great deal of interest, I assure you. The night before I left was our monthly consecration meeting. Several were obliged to be absent, and the excuses they sent were very helpful. I remember Fred Burton wrote, 'I am sorry not to be able to be with you this evening, but the Master's work calls me in another direction. Young Philips is very low, and I must stay with him tonight. May I ask that he have the prayers of the meeting?' And Lucy Reynolds wrote, 'Illness keeps me at home tonight, but my heart is with you.' Oh, we have such good times in our Christian Endeavor Society, Mattie!" and Lily launched into a full account of their doings at home, which continued till she bade them good night.

The minister heard no more. He had a new thought which must be turned over in his mind. He was his own cheerful self the next morning, and seemed to have forgotten all about his small prayer meeting.

The days slipped by pleasantly enough, and Sunday dawned. The congregation had just settled themselves into sermonful repose. The minister was reading the last notice, as they supposed—that same old one about the weekly prayer meeting which had grown so familiar that it seemed to go in one ear and out of the other. But Mr. Murray did not open the Bible and announce his text as they expected he would do. Instead, he stepped a little farther toward the front of the platform, and said, "Will all the members of the church who are unable for any reason to be present at the prayer meeting this week, please send an excuse in writing, on or before Wednesday evening, that it may be read at the meeting. It will be very pleasant to feel that we have the prayers and sympathy of the friends who are obliged to be absent. Any excuse which we can conscientiously give to the Lord Jesus Christ will answer the purpose, and will give those of the members who are present the feeling that your heart is with us, although your body cannot be there."

Only these few words, and he opened the Bible and announced the text they had waited for; but they did not hear it. They were a startled audience, or perhaps it would be better to say a company of startled individuals; for those who were in the habit of staying away from meeting of course did not know who else stayed away too, unless they were in their own family or their own immediate circle of friends, and so considered themselves, and not the whole congregation, addressed. Mr. Murray might have recited the Shorter Catechism, or a few pages of the dictionary or encyclopedia, that morning, so far as his sermon was heard by some of his audience.

Deacon Eldred, not being hit, went to sleep as usual. Poor old Father Fisk never understood the sermons. Mrs. Moker was deaf, and the Brunig sisters were not there. Mrs. Murray was too much occupied in imagining what people would think about Mr. Murray to give much time to the sermon, though it was one of his very best; and Miss Lily was very much occupied in studying the faces about her, and finding out what people did think.

Mrs. Hannibal Humphrey, under her new spring bonnet, was thinking something like this, "The perfect idea! Send an excuse to him! What business is it of his, I should like to know, what my excuse is for staying home from prayer meeting?" She kept herself strictly to that point; for it was rather uncomfortable to think back to last Wednesday night, and see herself leisurely reading an intensely interesting book. However, she was ready for this point if her conscience should bring it up. She might say that the book had to go back to the library the next day, and would require the evening to finish it, and she had no other time in which to read it. But her conscience did not bring it up. It knew it was of no use. Close by her side sat Mr. Hannibal Humphrey. He was not a member of the church. He did not consider himself included in the request that the new minister had made; but he thought it immensely amusing, and occupied the remainder of the hour in trying to frame an excuse for his wife. He often wrote responses to invitations for her, and on the way home he asked whether she would have it read.

My dear Pastor,
I am obliged to be absent from prayer meeting this evening, as we are invited to a small company at Mrs. Sullivan's, to meet their friend Miss Rochester, who is to leave town the next day. I am sorry I am unable to meet with you; but you see how it is.
Very truly,
Mrs. Hannibal Humphrey

Or did she intend, after all, to send regrets to Mrs. Sullivan's, and have the card party she had spoken of that morning? In that case it should read:

Dear Mr. Murray,
I am sorry to be absent from the meeting Wednesday evening; but we have arranged to have a few friends to spend the evening, and have a quiet game of cards. I should be glad to have you and Mrs. Murray step in after meeting.
Very truly,
Mrs. Hannibal Humphrey

"Perhaps, though," he said, as he handed her gravely the slip from his hymnbook, on which he had written the sample notes during the closing prayer, "it would be as well to leave off that closing sentence, as the thing is to be read in the meeting, and some of the rest might feel hurt unless they were invited too." But for some reason Mrs. Humphrey seemed not to wish to talk upon the subject, and told her husband that she thought he was very irreverent, whereat he laughed long and loud, disturbing Mrs. Humphrey's feelings still more.

Miss Effie Summers was a church member, but she could hardly remember when she had been to prayer meeting. Her aimless little mind began to search about for a reason why she had never been, and she had to admit to herself that it was because she had never thought of it. She almost smiled in church at the idea of herself at prayer meeting. It had never occurred to her as a place where she would care to go. She looked down at her gloves, and admired their fit, and wondered if, after all, the ones with the darker stitching on the backs would have been a better match to her suit, and remembered that it was last Wednesday afternoon that she had bought them; and that she had lounged in a big chair all the evening, eating cream-dates and talking nothings with her young cousin who chanced to come in, and never once thought there was a prayer meeting. She made her silly little heart keep still by telling it that not thinking of a thing was a good excuse for not doing it, although there was a slight question somewhere which interfered with the satisfaction she felt in the fit of her gloves, and made her wonder whether she would like to stand up before the great God and offer that excuse.

Mr. Worcester, just at her left, a tall, stern man of business, dismissed the prayer meeting subject with these words: "I really haven't time for prayer meeting. My hands are too full of business cares. I go to church on Sunday, and I'm sure I give a great deal to support the gospel, and that is all that can be expected of such a busy man as I am"; and his mind went off to a certain knotty point that he had not been quite able to decide the day before.

Will Kenton glanced uneasily over at Effie Summers. He was a member of the church too; but he had arranged it in his sleek little head that very morning that he would call upon Miss Effie Wednesday evening, and secure her company to the concert before that fellow from Boston got ahead of him. Miss Effie wouldn't be likely to go to prayer meeting. To be sure, he didn't go often enough himself to know who went, but he knew her well enough to hazard a guess. Effie looked very pretty, and there was no other evening on which to call; for Monday evening was his club, and Tuesday was the whist party. Just then the new glove went up to see if the new hat was straight, and the hand looked so very pretty that it carried the day. Then he told himself he really must go this time, and he would try and arrange for the prayer meeting another week.

Tired little Mrs. Carroll heard the request with dismay. Here was something else that ought to have been done. She was so overcrowded with cares that she didn't know which way to turn now. She thought back to last Wednesday night. She had just finished the twenty-seventh tuck in Lucy's white organdy that afternoon, and was so tired she could hardly finish the tea dishes. She sat back easier then. It surely wasn't her duty to go to prayer meeting when she was so tired it would have made her sick; yet she wondered dimly in her weary brain if, after all, that tuck hadn't been to blame, and whether she had any right to get so tired before the meeting. Would she like to present a tuck as her excuse to the Lord for not having attended his meeting? Her heart was not at rest. There was another sister who remembered herself as having been too tired to go last Wednesday; and she wondered if it would be necessary, in order to be strictly true, to say that she had been making pound cake all afternoon.

Mr. Mosley remembered with grim satisfaction that he had had the neuralgia last Wednesday, and had not thought it prudent to go out in the evening air; but he forgot that half an hour after the bell had ceased ringing he had gone to the door with Mr. Patterson, who had called on business, and there he had stood for a full fifteen minutes in a chill east wind, without so much as an overcoat or hat to protect him.

There were many who did not think at all, and who forgot the minister's request almost as soon as it was made, who had no idea of going to prayer meeting, and who did not know as they ever would have. There was one young lady who declared on the way home that she never went to prayer meetings, because she did not enjoy them. She thought they were poky places, and made one feel awfully doleful. Her brother told her he thought that was an excellent reason—and would she like to have him write the excuse for her? He would get it up in fine style; and he thought it would be better than most of the excuses other folks would write, because it was true, and no made-up reason. "All the same, Lou," said he, "I can't say I would like to give it to the One who is to test your excuses." Then he whistled. He had never said anything so solemn as that in his whole life before, and he did not exactly know his own voice. And the sister said, "Oh, nonsense!" but she did some thinking on the way home.

There was much talk at the various dinner tables of that congregation that day. Some thought the new pastor had taken a good deal upon him, and that he had no right to make such a request. "I suppose I might 'a' let the horses rest 'a' Wednesday afternoon, and not plowed the medder lot till Thursday," said Farmer Stevens, as he took a bite of pork, and shoveled some beans into his mouth with his knife. "We ain't been to prayer meeting in a good while. I reckon we'd better try to go this week." Meek little Mrs. Stevens' face brightened, and she said she'd be real glad to go. She had missed the prayer meeting, but she had never said so, and they lived so far out she hadn't thought it possible for them to go.

The Haines household discussed the matter at the dinner table. Little Nannie sat and listened, and, after turning it over in her mind for a time, bluntly asked of her elder sister, "Kit, why didn't you go to prayer meeting last Wednesday night? Oh, I remember! Your bonnet had just come home, and you didn't like it, and tore it all to pieces to fix it over. Wouldn't it 'a' been funny if you had written to Mr. Murray, 'Please excuse me from going to the meeting, 'cause my bonnet don't look right, and I have to trim it over'?" Amid the general laughter that followed, Miss Kittie told her sister she was a saucy little thing, and went to her room to quiet her upset nerves. There were some few who spent the Sunday afternoon hours in serious thought and in making many resolves which meant much for the future of that church prayer meeting.

Sunday passed, and Monday and Tuesday. Wednesday came; the sun went down behind some lovely clouds, and the moon sailed out, with here and there some attendant blinking stars, and the bell for evening worship pealed out. The minister took his Bible under his arm, waited a moment for his wife and Lily to pass out, then locked the door; and together they went down the street. Mrs. Murray felt decidedly nervous. Miss Lily, also, was a little excited, for from the other direction, she could see the two Burnside girls with their brother, and she couldn't help wondering whether it could be possible that they were coming to the meeting. But Mr. Murray walked silently along, not joining in the little hum of talk that his wife and her sister kept up. He was thinking of what he was to say to his people, and he felt no nervousness about the meeting; for he had spent much time in prayer that afternoon, and he knew that the meeting was in the hands of his heavenly Father, to prosper as he would.

Early as they were, when they opened the door they saw the long rows of usually empty seats nearly filled, and more people were coming down the street. Lily noticed in surprise that the Burnsides were really coming up the steps. Various forces had combined to bring these people there.

Miss Effie Summers was there because she had not anything to do, and it was a lovely night, and she had thought of it, and there really was not any reason why she should not go, just for once, and she supposed she ought to go sometimes, anyway. Besides, it troubled her to think that she would need to present her excuse to the Lord. So she was there, and, upon being whispered with for a few minutes, reluctantly consented to preside at the organ. Will Kenton came in a little late, and somewhat flurried, having been to call upon Miss Effie; but upon being told that she had gone to meeting, he, in much amazement, had bowed himself out, and made his way to the church.

Mrs. Hannibal Humphrey was not there; but she had an excuse. She was neither at Mrs. Sullivan's tea party, nor entertaining company herself. Instead, she had retired to a dark room with a sick-headache. Her unfeeling husband told her she had good taste, for he thought on the whole it would sound much better than either of the excuses he had written. However, she sent no excuse. Mr. Humphrey was there himself. It came about in this way. He had lounged around in the room, and read all the papers through, and it seemed very dull. Supper eaten all alone was a gloomy affair, and Mrs. Humphrey did not seem inclined to talk when he went up to see her. Then the church bell rang; and the thought came, why should he not go to meeting? He believed he would go, just to see if there would be any excuses, and what they would be, and who would be there. He might be able to get some fun out of it; it certainly was dull enough at home. So he went.

Mr. Worcester was there because all the plans he had laid out for that evening came to naught. The man with whom he had made an appointment sent word he could not come; the book he had intended reviewing he had forgotten, and left in his downtown office; and the letters he had thought to answer did not come at all, the mail-train being delayed by an accident. The bell rang, and Mr. Worcester in despair took himself to the Lord's house.

Mr. Mosley did not have the neuralgia; and, being a prominent member of the church, he thought it would not do to utterly ignore the new pastor's request, and so he went. Mrs. Carroll dragged her weary self to the church because her conscience troubled her for having allowed Lucy to coax her into buying her a dark-blue surah, and she hoped to find some peace of mind in going as a sort of penance. Not that she put it that way. She would have been shocked if you had suggested such a thing, and she kept it strictly a secret from her better self. The pound cake woman even refrained from making an elaborate dish for tea that night so that she might come to the meeting.

There were of course the few faithful ones who always came to prayer meeting when they could, because they loved it, and because the Lord had promised to meet his children there and bless them; but they were not so very many.

And so, for various reasons, these people had taken their bodies up to the house of the Lord to spend a little time in communion with him; and the Lord looked and saw the hearts all taken up with the cares of this world, and longed to bless them, but saw that some minds were far from his church and his worship.

At the door, Father Fisk, who acted as sexton, handed Mr. Murray two notes. One was crumpled, misspelled, and nearly illegible.

Dear Mr. Murray,

I am laid up with the rumatiz, and can't com to the meetin', but my heart is with you. May the Lord be there. Your humble servant,

Susan Moker

The other was from Deacon Eldred, written in a trembling hand.

Dear Pastor,

My precious wife who has traveled beside me for so many years has passed on before. I trust I may have the prayers of God's people tonight in my deep sorrow.

Oh, that meeting! It was a revelation to some of those who didn't usually attend.

"I never dreamed a prayer meeting could be so interesting!" said Miss Effie merrily, as she laid her hand on young Will Kenton's arm, on the way down the church steps after meeting. She had been prevailed upon to play the organ, and she had done it well. Will Kenton's rich tenor had swelled out with Mr. Hannibal Humphrey's bass, and carried other voices in such a tide of song as astonished the old church walls.

The minister's few words seemed to stir his audience as it had not been stirred in many a long year. A few repeated verses. One lady called for a favorite hymn. Mr. Worcester was moved to pray for Deacon Eldred in his great sorrow, and others followed.

They went out from that hour of prayer feeling as if they had received a blessing, and wanted to come again. Some wondered why they had never gone before.

Lily lingered in the parlor with her sister to talk over the meeting, and exult over the appearance of this one and that.

But the minister, alone in the moonlit study, knelt and thanked God.

JOHN CHAMBERLAIN'S
EASTER COAT

*I*T was Monday morning, and the world had put on its workaday clothes again, and started the busy song of the week. Even the lazy clouds, which but the day before had been still and dreamy in their Sunday quiet, seemed to be scurrying across the sky with a purpose. The whiz and whir of machinery from the tannery and sawmill across the river could be heard distinctly. Everything seemed to be bustling about to get ready for spring to come. The withered grass, amid patches of dirty, discouraged looking snow that seemed about ready to take its departure, spruced up a little, and actually tried to send forth a faint green tinge in response to the warm sunlight.

A young man, a salesman perhaps, walked briskly down the street of the little village toward the two stores, with a large valise in his hand. He had a business air, even to the slightest detail of his dress. His nicely fitting clothes reminded one of the bustling city.

But despite all the atmosphere of hurry that hung over the place, John Chamberlain still stood at his front gate. He was watching the young man, presumably a salesman, as he hastened down the street. It was not so much the man, either, that his eyes were fixed upon, as it was his clothes. Any one could tell by a glance at those clothes that they were made by a city tailor, and they gave their wearer an air of grace and importance which John Chamberlain's clothes had never afforded. He knew the lines of that coat on the young man almost as well as his own; for he had studied their shape with careful eye during the whole of the sermon yesterday morning, envying the turn of the collar, and even the two jaunty buttons set behind. He looked down again at his own coat as the other disappeared within a store at the end of the street. What was it but an ungainly covering which always made him feel that his hands were encumbrances which were to be got along with the best way he could; that his joints were made of wood, and would not move at his bidding; and that his whole figure was utterly out of proportion in every direction?

He wished he could have a coat made by a real city tailor himself. He had never had one. Money was scarce. He despised these cheap, ready-made affairs he had worn since he had grown too old for his mother to make his clothes. He took out his knife, and cut spiteful little chips out of the fence post. Why should that fellow—meaning, of course, the salesman—wear such coats with that insolent, easy way, and he, John Chamberlain, have to wear these nasty store-made things that he despised? He had been given a good education, if he was poor, and the salesman did not look as if he had any brains worth mentioning. Yet Jessie had cast actual glances of admiration in his direction after church, and asked who he was. Of course the admiration was for the coat. Jessie was such a stylish, trim little thing! Here his face grew tender as the vision of the slender, dainty, bright-faced girl came before him—Jessie, who always seemed to be able to make a pretty costume out of almost nothing. Her clothes, nevertheless, made her look utterly unlike any of the other girls of the village, and set her well above them so far as style, though the others tried hard to eclipse her. His heart rebelled against a fact that kept him from having a coat that would merit admiration from Jessie. He felt sure he would be able to walk up the church aisle with as much nonchalance as the young stranger if he could wear the stranger's clothes, and not let his hands and feet get in the way.

There was much nicking of the fence post done that morning, for John Chamberlain was deciding an important question; but it was settled at last, and he started for his work. He walked down the street briskly, too, now. He had decided to have a new coat; and, once decided, it was almost as good as having it on his back that minute. Why, there was the entire variety of coats to choose from—Prince Alberts, sack-coats, business coats, and the whole world of coats! An evening suit even hovered dimly on the horizon of his mind, without any shadow of an idea of coming nearer to him, however; but it was pleasant

to him to think of it as a possibility. He walked down
that street in all the glory of the best-fitting clothes
that the finest city tailor could make. His arms
swung easily at his sides, and he was for once utterly
unconscious of the red, bony appendages which he
used for hands, and which had hitherto troubled him
so much. Imagination can do a great deal. It even
went so far as to make him raise his arm, covered at
that moment with the prospective Prince Albert
sleeve, which was to be bound with braid, and finished with two small, neat buttons, and touch his
hat with as much grace of movement as a city salesman could possibly use, to Jessie as he passed her
house; and she thought as she blushingly returned
the salute, "What a fine figure John has! Strange I
never noticed before how handsome he is growing!"

If he was going to have the coat, he might as well
have it at once, he thought. In two weeks it would
be the Easter vacation. Jessie's two brothers would
be at home then for a few days, and she had said she
wanted to have a little gathering for them. It would
be very nice to have something new for that time.
Indeed, now he thought of it, it was absolutely
necessary that he have it for church on Easter Sunday. Why, it would be very embarrassing to have to
attend church under the eyes of those college
brothers with his old, ill-shaped coat! It certainly
would not do. He would go down to the city the very
next day and have his measurements taken, that the
new one might be ready in time. This much settled,
he went to his work with a light heart, and whistling
a joyous tune. All day long as he went about his

duties he saw himself as he would appear in the new garment. He felt the pleasure with which he would enter the church. It would be an unusual time, anyway. The church would be trimmed, and all the ladies would have their spring bonnets. John had a dim idea that a new bonnet was in some way connected with Easter time; and if bonnets, why not coats? Of course he must look his best. He would feel that he fitted in with the flowers and the extra music and all the gala attire, if he had his new coat.

But about the resurrection of Jesus Christ, that most marvelous of all the proofs that God has given us of his love and mercy, that wonderful story which makes us sure that we shall never die, John thought not one whit that day. Easter to him was a time of wearing new clothes; a time of the return of college brothers; a time of enjoyment that held all sorts of delightful possibilities for him. Not that he was not a Christian, this young man whose heart at that present moment seemed to be given over to dress. Why, he was to lead the young people's prayer meeting on that eventful Easter Sunday night; but he had forgotten about that entirely. When it did again enter his consciousness, it looked to him like a tremendous cross—especially under the existing circumstances of possibly sarcastic college brothers—which must be taken up and carried in the easiest way. Nevertheless, it would be easier if carried on the shoulders of a new coat. He could even think of himself quite composedly, as standing up before the desk in his new coat announcing a hymn.

On the whole, that meeting had a pleasant side to

it; for after the cross had been borne and the meeting was over, he might persuade Jessie to let him walk home with her; and perhaps, if the evening was pleasant, and the moonlight bright, she would not mind walking on up the hill a little way. And then, *perhaps*—it *might* be—that he would feel the time had come to say something to Jessie which he had long wanted to say. It would all depend upon the effect of the new coat.

So the young fellow worked and whistled away, and thought his pleasant thoughts; and the night at last came when he could dream them all over again; and then the morning, with an early breakfast, and a rush for the fast express that would take him to the city in an hour and a half.

Then began a day for John. He had not imagined it would be so hard a task to do his shopping. He went from tailor to tailor, seeking exactly the coat of his ideal; but it proved hard to find, at least at the price he could afford to pay, for this young fellow had extravagant tastes, although he did not know it. They showed him one after another, and tried to make him think he would have a ready-made one; but he was firm. A coat made to order he would have, and no other; and at last, after weary searchings, he found the right piece of cloth, corresponding both to the size of his purse and his taste. It was with pride that he doffed his old coat that his measurements might be taken; and he drew his fine proportions up to their full height, and looked down upon himself as the tape measure went grimly around his chest. Soon he would have a coat that he could be proud of; and this tape measure was its harbinger, and, therefore, a badge of honor. Of course he did not really think all this, or at least did not realize that he was so doing, for John was a young man of too good sense to have said all this to himself; but there was the pleasant sensation of it in his soul which made him lean back in his seat in the home-ward-bound evening train, and actually enjoy his ride home, weary though he was with his shopping.

With thoughts of himself in his new attire, John's days dragged slowly by until it should be done; and as the important Sunday drew near, he began to be anxious lest it would not be done in time. But the coat arrived from the tailor's, and Jessie's brothers from their college, on the same train on Saturday evening. John met them both at the station, a little chagrined, it is true, that he had to wear his old coat; but it was dark, and he kept well in the shadow. Besides, he felt a sort of gentle, stylish influence from the bundle under his arm, even through its several heavy wrappings. With the knowledge of what was inside that brown paper he could walk easily beside even college-bred young men.

They beguiled him into a scheme for the evening, the brothers and Jessie; and he came home rather late, the precious package still unwrapped, only to remember as he entered his room that he was the leader of the meeting for the following evening, and that he had not prepared for it in the slightest degree. He took down his Bible, and tried to make some little preparation then; but his eyes were heavy, and he soon gave it up. He had to have one look at his coat before his head touched the pillow. He untied the strings, and drew it from the paper; but just as he held it at arm's length, and shook out the folds, his kerosene lamp, which his landlady did not believe in filling very often, flickered and sputtered, and its gasping flame sank lower and lower. He turned it up impatiently, and tried to look again closely at the coat; but the flickering flame winked lugubriously, and gave warning that it would last but a moment more, and he had better hasten to his bed or he would be left in utter darkness to make his final preparations. He laid the coat carefully on his chair, and made all haste to obey, feeling it a little hard that he should be thus prevented from a scrutinizing view of this long-awaited garment. But he smiled as he turned out the light of the wicked, smoking lamp, and said to himself, "Never mind. It will be there in the morning. I can wait, and I'll enjoy it all the better then."

Then he went to sleep to dream of the pleasant evening he had passed, and of the morrow that might be so full of joy for him.

It was late when he awoke the next morning. The first early church bell was actually ringing. He sprang up, and dressed hastily, not caring to put on the new apparel until after he had been down to breakfast. Back in his room, he hastened at last to the coat. There it lay in all the glory of its newness and its supposed city fit. Its color was so very black and its buttons so very precise and trim, that he felt like apologizing for the blacking on his boots, brushed to a high polish though it was.

On went the coat; for there really was not much time left for admiration, if one was to get to the church before the whole congregation was seated. He buttoned the last button proudly, and stepped to the glass to survey himself.

Oh, horror of horrors! What was this? A cold chill began to creep upward, and a heavy feeling replaced his happiness. Could it be that it did not fit? What! A city coat not fit! A coat cut by a city tailor *not fit!* Why, no one ever heard of such a thing! There must be some mistake. He must have put it on wrong in some way. He gave it a decided yank upward, and then smoothed it over his shoulders with both hands, as a lady does with an ill-fitting dress, and then squared about again in defiance to the glass. But no; the collar sagged down in the back with the same dogged air as before. With despair he seized hold of the shoulders of the innocent thing, and gave it such a jerk toward his ears as could not fail to bring about a decided change in the set of the article. But the more fiercely he pulled and smoothed and raised his shoulders and ducked his head forward in his attempts, the more determined that collar grew to lop out and away from the shining linen it was meant to cover. The linen collar creaked and squeaked, the shirt bosom groaned, the necktie writhed itself till the bow was under one ear; but all to no purpose.

Disappointment was no name for the feeling in John's heart. He had not realized how thoroughly he had come to depend upon this new coat, nor how much his heart had been set upon it. If he had been a girl he would have cried; but being a man he did not understand himself, and his face grew red, and he tore around his room and glared at his crooked, cracked looking-glass. To add to his confusion, the second bell for church began to ring, and soon he knew it would toll. He tried to calm himself, for certainly this coat must be worn to church if he went at all. It would not do to wear the old one after all the abuse he had heaped upon it during the week. He tried another collar not quite so high, and then one higher, a darker necktie too; but all seemed to make no difference. He brushed his hair over again savagely two or three times; but still his head continued to look as if it were going on ahead of him, with that coat collar like a rudder steering him. At last the bell was almost done tolling; he seized his hat and rushed down the street to the church, arriving there out of breath just as the choir began the opening anthem.

John Chamberlain thought as he entered the church and searched about for a seat—and none was to be found—that the eyes of the whole congregation were upon him and his coat collar. If he had seen the tailor who made it, I am not sure but he would have strangled him then and there. He remembered with mortification the delight with which he had contemplated himself in his mind's eye in this very coat; and now the reality was causing him more embarrassment than he had known in all the time he had owned his old one. Why, he had been well pleased with that when it was new. He had not expected anything better of it than to cover him and to look clean and new. He realized with a sense of pain that this one best coat of his which was to him so much, had been just a common, everyday affair to the tailor who made hundreds of them for common use by the city people. His painful thoughts were interrupted by hearing the announcement of the young people's meeting that evening; and he experienced that sudden, awful feeling that he was rushing on to a moment for which he was not prepared and for which he seemed to have lost all power to prepare.

But there did come a calm in this whirl of thoughts. It was during the singing, "I know that my Redeemer lives." The triumphant melody floated over the church, and John Chamberlain could but listen; for it was as if angels had charge of that music, and were wafting it to hearts, and not alone to ears. He did not understand why the thought that his Redeemer had risen thrilled him just then as it never had done before. Perhaps it was because the dear Lord was present there, ready to come to each troubled or doubting heart, even to John Chamberlain, sitting there in his new, disappointing coat, in the back seat, with his head bowed.

Surely he did come and bless that heart, for John felt a peace which he had not known before. It did not come from the sermon, for that was not so very wonderful, though John thought it was; but it must have been from the Master himself, for it stayed with him. John could not have told much of the sermon when it was over. Indeed, he felt very uncertain about the text. He only knew that he had been with the disciples as they took the body of Jesus from the cross and prepared it for the burial. He fancied he himself had helped to pour out the precious spices; he felt the sorrow in his heart, all the while, that the disciples must have felt when they thought they were doing the last bit of service for their Master; and then he seemed to have stood afar off and watched the stone as it was rolled to the opening in the tomb and a great seal set upon it. It was all very vivid to him. He was certain he knew how the disciples felt when the angel spoke to them; for the angel seemed to have spoken to him, and said, "Fear not, for he is risen." And after that he seemed to have talked with the Master himself.

The prayer which followed the sermon seemed to John to be conversation with a risen, present Savior, and not a talk addressed to a God afar off, as prayer usually seemed to him. He had forgotten his coat utterly. He was uplifted.

Jessie noticed him as he sat listening with earnest, attentive gaze to the speaker. John was a handsome man, she thought, as she turned back to listen herself, and see what it was in which he appeared to be so much interested. She had not seen the ill fit of the coat collar, and was not sufficiently versed in coats to know that it was wrong if she had. John looked nice in her eyes, and she was glad.

Instead of going to walk as was John's custom on Sunday afternoons, and dropping in at Jessie's house perhaps, he stayed in his room. He felt that he had much to think about, and must be by himself. There was the meeting. It could not be passed by easily. After the impression the morning sermon made upon his heart, he did not dare to stand up there and lead the meeting in a perfunctory manner as he ordinarily did when it came his turn, without saying one word upon the subject himself, nor even leading in prayer, but rather calling upon someone else to do it for him, and shirking every possible duty that he could. For a little while that afternoon he felt that he must go to someone and say that he could not lead the meeting, he felt so unworthy; but the same Spirit that had been with him in the morning led him to a different frame of mind, until he was willing to kneel down and say, "Here, Lord, am I, unworthy though I am. Make me useful as thou wilt."

The new coat hung carelessly over a chair, forgotten while the owner studied his Bible. When John Chamberlain once more donned his proud apparel, there was indeed a slight feeling of regret and disappointed hopes connected with it; but it seemed of very little consequence now, in the light of the last few hours. One glance he gave at himself in the glass just before he left the room; and really the collar was not quite so bad after all, but lay almost meekly about his neck. He went down the street clothed not in fine raiment, as he had hoped to be, but in the quiet garment of humility. One thought was in his mind now, not of earthly apparel, but of spiritual; an old thought, which Paul expressed in these words: "For in this we groan, earnestly desiring to be clothed upon with our house which is from heaven ... that mortality might be swallowed up of life."

"Now is Christ risen from the dead, and become the first fruits of them that slept." He could almost hear the words of the morning song echoing yet in his heart; and it brought new meaning to him now as he realized that he, too, would one day arise to be with Christ forever. Over and over in his mind ran the words, as he took that walk in the starlight while the bells chimed their joyful resurrection carols, "So when this corruptible shall have put on incorruption, and this mortal shall have put on immortality, then shall be brought to pass the saying that is written, Death is swallowed up in victory."

John and Jessie took that walk together after the service, just as he had thought they might. She had meant to stop at her own gate, of course. When they had reached it, John had been talking so earnestly about the meeting, and there had been such a longing in her own heart not to have the talk end, that she had yielded when he held her arm a little more firmly and said, "Just let us walk a little farther, Jessie; I'm not half through talking yet."

On they walked, not heeding how far after that; out where the road melted into still green fields, with mossy, sleepy-looking fences on either side; out where the soft gray clouds sweep overhead and do not look, and even the little trees by the roadside are asleep and cannot hear.

They had many things to talk about, for the meeting had been a very helpful one, and this was a resurrection day to these two hearts in more ways than one. Jessie felt how cold-hearted a Christian she had been for a long time, and she told John she meant to be different now; that he had helped her to some new thoughts which she would never forget, and that Christ was more to her than he had ever been before; and John felt his heart throb with joy and gratitude that, though he was unworthy, he had been used by the Master so soon.

Yes, and he did speak those words he had thought so long to speak, all unfitting as his coat collar was. I am not sure, though, that he would have dared to do so even in the glories of the salesman's stylish suit, if a cloud had not covered the moon often that night, and if his heart had not been so warm and happy about other things, that such small, insignificant objects as coats vanished into oblivion.

In due course of time, when the pain of the disappointment had disappeared, John told Jessie all about it, and she laughed with him, and cried about it too; for her true woman's heart saw between his comical sentences the keen disappointment he must have felt over the failure of his first "dress-up" coat to be all he had planned it should be. But when the laugh was over, and they were quietly and soberly talking about it, she said, "John, I'm glad it didn't fit, after all; for then you might have been complacent, and never come to have that wonderful feeling about the resurrection of Jesus Christ which filled you so full that it reached even to me. Dress is one of the things that leads people away from Christ. It must be one of the greatest things he meant when he said, 'Come out from among them, and be ye separate.' It always did seem dreadful to me to talk about Easter bonnets, as if they had any connection with the resurrection of Jesus Christ. Easter coats are not any worse than Easter bonnets, John; but I am glad it didn't fit."

A VOICE
UNHEARD

*T*HE sun was just bidding good night to a little summer resort, brushing its lake with many colors, lighting up the windows of its cottages, touching with glory its tallest treetops, and making that particular spot feel as if there were no other spot on earth quite so beautiful or so beloved by the sun. The lake had a peculiar look, as if it had been sweeping itself into small eddies just as the sun went down, and had caught itself in the act, and stood motionless to watch the light of his dying. One small sailboat, with its still white sail, lay upon the surface, and drifted so softly you would have thought it was becalmed. A little steamer going on its necessary evening journey seemed to ply its wheels more quietly, and to hush its noisy breathing, as if the place and the sight might be desecrated thereby. Two or three cranes whirled low and slow above the calm water, as though performing some solemn priestly office. It was plain that the sun had caught and held the attention of the earth and its creatures; for even the little birds hushed their chirpings, as with invisible hand the wonderful colors of the sky were changed, now from a delicate yellow—the light that would come from the sun shining through a bit of amber—into a suggestion of emeralds seen through a flood of glory light, then a flash of a rosy-colored banner above, to blend with the soft gray clouds into the deeper purple, and to grow into scarlet and dark crimson as the sun sank lower.

Only a few human witnesses were there that night, for it was late in the season. In fact, the season was already over, and there was but a handful of people remaining of all the throng who had visited that popular resort during the summer. The place seemed desolate now—so many cottages closed. It made the few lingerers long to seek the sunset every night as something which would be just as grand for its few observers as it had been all summer long for the crowds that had sought the summer-house on the summit of the hill by the lake. The summer-house, or observatory as it was called, had no flaring paint to mar the beauty of the scene, making gaudy attempt to vie with the sunset. It was of the soft gray tint that the wind and the sun and the rain spread over what is left them to paint. The human watchers were, for the most part, silent too, though one of them hummed softly to himself, "More love to thee, O Christ," until it seemed as if the song were a part of the sweet night air, breathing the very words into each heart.

By and by the sky became more muted, and the evening star peeped shyly out, looking around to see if the sun could anywhere be seen, and then glowing more brightly as it gained courage. Soon over the water sounded the tones of the church bell. But it seemed, though sweet and clear, only halfhearted in its call; and it may be that the ringer was at fault, for the sound did not invite joyfully, but slowly told of duty ahead.

"Why, it is prayer meeting night!" said one of the lingerers at the sunset, reluctantly drawing out his watch. Surely, they had all forgotten! But why was it that the thought of the little church did not seem as pleasant as this place where they had felt so near to God? Could it be that, as they went slowly down the hill, with many a lingering look at the fading light, they actually had a thought that God was sending them away to do some disagreeable duty for him?

Be that as it may, it seemed as though they did not all take his Spirit with them as they came straggling by ones and twos into the prayer meeting room. The room itself was not naturally of a cheerful disposition; and its air, from confinement during the week, had become musty and dusty. Whoever acted as sexton seemed not to think it worthwhile to light up much for so few people; for the kerosene lamps, set on brackets very high upon the wall, had to exert themselves as much as their turned-down condition would allow in order to make any light at all through their cloudy chimneys.

There were but two singing books in the room, one on the pulpit and one shut up in the organ. The regular pastor of the church was away, and had asked a brother minister who was there on his vacation to lead in his place. One smoky lamp stood on the desk to glare unflinchingly into his eyes, and make him appear like a dark specter to the people in front who were trying to see him. There were several good musicians there; but the leader did not appear to know it, for he looked despairingly at the vacant organ stool, and then after whispered consultations with one or two near him, who all shook their heads emphatically said, "Is there someone present who will preside at the organ and help in the singing?"

Deep silence ensued. There was a young man near the organ who played in his own church at home. He looked at the instrument and then at the minister, hesitated, looked again, and finally sat still. So did everyone else.

The minister gave out a hymn, carefully announcing twice the number and page, utterly unconscious of the fact that he was the only one in the room who possessed a book. He looked about once more encouragingly, in the hope that someone would appear to play; but as no one did, he said, "Will someone kindly lead us in the singing?" Dead silence again.

A young lady in the audience looked down at her toes, and thought to herself that perhaps she might start the tune if she was perfectly certain no one else would start out at the same time, and come into collision with her. She began thinking the tune over to herself, to see whether it would be too high if she should start; but the thought of it all had made her heart beat so fast that she concluded she should choke and break down if she tried, so she gave over the effort. The minister looked worried. He could not sing himself, poor man, or thought he could not, which served the same purpose. At last, just as he was about to make one more appeal, a dear old sister with a very cracked voice started the tune in a very high key. Such of the congregation as could climb high enough accompanied her, though she had it pretty much her own way through some parts of the verse. The minister noticed the scarcity of the music, and, looking about for a cause, discovered the lack of books. At the close of the hymn he remarked that he was sorry there were no more books, but that they would sing familiar hymns, and try to do their best, if everyone would help.

Now, there sat a boy in that room, who knew that not ten feet away from him was a closet door behind which were a hundred copies just like the singing book which the minister held; and yet he did not stir from his seat to get them. Perhaps he did not think, or the distance from his seat to that door looked very long, or it might be that his boots squeaked, or he did not care about the singing, anyway.

The minister prayed at length in heavy sentences, and not with his usual warmth. The singing had somehow depressed him. It had been labor instead of praise. After the prayer came the reading of the chapter. There having been no regular topic for the evening announced, he had selected the thirteenth chapter of John, where Jesus talks with his faithful ones about the new commandment of love which he gives to them, which shall be the sign by which all men shall know that they are his disciples. Then they labored with another hymn, after which the leader made some remarks upon the chapter he had read; but the audience seemed to have almost forgotten what it was about, for they listened with a dreamy sort of air that showed their whole minds were not upon the subject.

At the close of a verse of another hymn, the meeting was thrown open for prayer. They all sat as if under a spell, until at last one good old man arose and prayed long and in a low tone, unheard by more than half of those present. The leader had hoped that this would start others: but no; when the old man sat down there ensued a silence more intense than before. "Will someone else lead us in prayer?" he asked with the feeling that a little push would set things going all right. But no one else seemed inclined to pray. There was no help in falling back upon the singing, for each new attempt seemed a worse failure than the last, until it was becoming a positive torture to the poor minister to announce anything. And so the meeting dragged its weary minutes away. Occasionally some one would make a monotonous, commonplace speech, or a prayer whose sentences were old and dead, and asked for nothing in particular; but there were, all the way through, those awful pauses, like yawning chasms, between everything that was said or sung or done.

It was not that they had no thoughts, these people who had brought their bodies without gladness up to the house of the Lord. One of those who had witnessed the sunset sat there, and his mind was filled with the glory of it still. He was thinking how like a Christian's death is the sunset, with its greatest glory and beauty coming at the end of its course. The idea interested him much; and he proceeded to carry it out in his mind, likening the whole course of the sun to the life of a Christian. It did occur to him to tell his thoughts to the meeting, but he could not seem to make anything he had to say fit the subject, and so he sat still; and it was a pity, for there were some there, hardworking people, in whose hearts the "world had been set" so firmly that they had almost forgotten that "He hath made everything beautiful in his time," and that the sunsets were given for them to look at, and from which to learn God's lessons.

There was a girl thinking over to herself with beating heart the words:

I was poor yesterday, but not today;
For Jesus came this morning
And took the poor away;
And he left the legacy
He promised long ago.
So peace and joy and love
Through all my being flow.

I was tired yesterday, but not today.
I could run and not be weary,
This blessed way;
For I have his strength to stay me,
With his might my feet are shod,
I can find my resting places
In the promises of God.

What if she should dare to repeat those verses? Perhaps they would not fit, after all, and she was in a strange place. It would be better for her to keep still. Nevertheless, as each painful pause occurred, her heart beat loudly, and told her many times that she was almost on the point of opening her mouth; but she did not.

One old elder talked of the new commandment, the love that ran all through the Bible. Near him sat a young man who was a musician. The week before he had been in Music Hall in his city home, and listened to the wonderful tones of the great pipe organ. Somehow his thoughts were carried back now to that music. He could hear the strains again. There was the deep-toned bass, the plaintive alto, the sweet tenor; but soaring high above all, clear and beautiful, came the soprano. Love was like that soprano, soaring above everything else, uplifting and bearing along. The thought seemed to the young man a good one, and he carried it out more fully; but only for his own benefit. He did not open his mouth for the others to hear. Several brethren had it in their hearts to pray; but when they considered the matter, there really did not seem to be much they could ask for except that the meeting might be blessed. It did not occur to them that they were doing their best to keep it from being a blessing to anyone, and that perhaps it was in their hands to make it a good one. However that was, they kept still.

"For I have loved thee with an everlasting love, therefore with lovingkindness have I drawn thee."

These words came to one present; and her heart told her to repeat them, and tell the others how God had verified that promise to her.

"He that hath my commandments, and keepeth them, he it is that loveth me; and he that loveth me shall be loved of my Father, and I will love him, and will manifest myself to him," thought another one of his disciples as she sat quietly in a shadowy corner.

"Behold what manner of love the Father hath bestowed upon us, that we should be called the sons of God." "God is love; and he that dwelleth in love dwelleth in God, and God in him." How the verses multiplied in the hearts of the worshipers! But they did not speak the words aloud.

An old lady during the lengthy pauses longed to call for her favorite hymn:

There's a wideness in God's mercy,
Like the wideness of the sea.
There's a kindness in his justice
Which is more than liberty.

But she remembered the difficulty with which they had sung even those that the leader had selected, and her courage failed her. By her side sat a young lady who could have sung that sweet hymn so that it would have sounded almost like angel music, for she had often done so; but neither of them knew, and so the meeting lost that. One man in the audience remembered the words of an eminent speaker whom he had once heard: "We are Christ's inheritance. What has he in us?" and thought of quoting the verses, "And when they had called the apostles, and beaten them, they commanded that they should not speak in the name of Jesus, and let them go. And they departed from the presence of the council, rejoicing that they were counted worthy to suffer shame for his name," with the added sentence, "That is what Jesus Christ had in those disciples; what has he in us?" He thought the sentences over so many times that they finally came to have very little force, and he concluded that they were better left unsaid. If he had but said those words, it might have roused some few disciples to the fact that they were far from following the example of those who rejoiced to be counted worthy to suffer from speaking "in his name," but were acting just as though someone had really commanded that they should not speak in the name of Jesus. No doubt Satan had, and they obeyed.

"Do not let the time run to waste," urged the leader; nevertheless, he would have been glad if it had "run" a little faster. Even the dragged-out singing did not take up much of it. Now and then he threw in a remark himself when the pauses were unbearable; but he was growing nervous, and his remarks seemed desultory. He was a young man, and it embarrassed him exceedingly to have a meeting that he led go in this way. It lacked a good ten minutes of the end of the hour when he at last arose and said with a sigh, "Well, if no one has anything to say we will close by singing, 'Nearer my God, to thee.' "

They sang it in the same laborious way they had used for all the other hymns, and the long drawn out,

"E'en though it be a cross," floated out from the church to sound to the chance passerby as though the people felt they were bearing that cross then and there, and that it was a heavy one. Then they bowed their heads, almost impatiently waiting for the parting words of blessing, and hastened out with a relieved air, as much as to say, "There! We have accomplished that for another week, and we are glad!"

Now, there had been no infidel in that meeting to sneer and go out to make fun of the church on account of it; but there were many who were half-hearted Christians, and all needed the help that a good prayer meeting would have given. There was even one soul who was questioning in her own mind whether there was anything desirable in religion, and had come that night with the intention of trying to find out; but before the evening was half over she had forgotten all about her interest in Christ, and was filling her mind with other things. No one else seemed to take any interest in the meeting, why should she?

There were some who needed the organ's story of love; some who needed the sunset's picture, and the verses that might have been repeated, or the songs that might have been sung. Of course there were. Why else should they have been put into the hearts of those present? The dim little cheerless chapel might have been filled with sacred thoughts and wonderful pictures for those of Christ's children who spent their winters in that place, and came up to the house to worship every week; and the old lady who did not quite approve of having an organ in the church would have looked at it in a new way, perhaps, if she had only heard it used as a simple yet beautiful illustration; and ever after she might have listened for its soprano notes, and thought of the wonderful love they have been used to symbolize.

Every soul in that room might have been uplifted if each one had done his part. They had forgotten the words, "Then they that feared the Lord spake often one to another; and the Lord hearkened and heard it, and a book of remembrance was written before him for them that feared the Lord and that thought upon his name."

What did the angels think as they watched? And the Lord hearkening, and hearing so little of what he had given to be said? How indifferent and unloving must his children have seemed that night! And the records of that meeting, could they have been written in that wonderful "book of remembrance"?

THE PLEDGE

*A*NEW assistant pastor came to the church on the avenue. He had progressive ideas and a brisk business manner, and the people hoped much from his coming. The dear old pastor was beloved by all, and was in hearty sympathy with new ideas that the young people might bring forward; but his eye was dim and his energy abated, and he was not able to give them the active service that they needed. So they looked to the vigorous younger man for help. The Young People's Society of Christian Endeavor was not in the most flourishing condition, and the few faithful workers who were determined that it should not die went to the younger pastor for advice. They looked to see his face kindle with the light of enthusiasm; but instead he looked at them rather coldly, and said, "Well, the fact is, my young friends, I don't believe in the Christian Endeavor Society. In the first place, I do not believe in pledges."

He launched into a long dissertation upon the evils of pledges; but the faithful few heard little of it. They looked into his face with surprise, and turned away with a sigh, feeling that in him they would find no helper to bring their pledge-breakers back into the fold.

"How is it that he believes in marriage, then?" asked one young woman, as they walked away sadly together. "He had to pledge his truth and honor and love."

"Or how can he urge people to unite with God's church, since they have to take such solemn vows upon themselves?" said the serious one, with troubled eyes.

"He can't do much business with such ideas," said the bright-faced boy, who always forgot to be respectful; "for how could he sign his name to a check? A check is a promise to pay."

"And what more is our Christian Endeavor pledge than a promise to pay to our God what we owe him?" added the serious one.

"Oh, he doesn't understand yet," gently put in the excuser, who always labored painfully to think the best of everyone, especially a minister of God. "The time will come when he will see."

This seemed like a prophecy. Then they sighed for the one that was gone forever from their midst, for they knew what she would have said just here, "We must pray"; and with one accord they went silently into a vacant Bible-class room, and knelt together, their hearts full of petition for help from the Fountainhead.

But since the society, though feeble, was already in existence, and was favored by the senior pastor, and since the pledges already made had been made to God and not to man, the society could not cease to exist. A meeting was called by the faithful few, which the senior pastor promised to attend; and, as there had been special effort made, nearly all whose names had ever been upon the society roll were present, as well as many who had never attended the meetings.

The president made an earnest little speech, an exhortation to the pledge-breakers to renew their vows, and to outsiders to join them. He gave opportunity for others to speak; and after a few minutes' silence a young man arose, and said that he had not joined the society because of the pledge, that he did not believe in pledges; but if they would do away with that feature of their organization, he would be glad to lend them his influence.

The kind eyes of the old pastor had kindled with righteous indignation during this speech; and when it was done he arose and said, "Dear friends, the young brother who has just spoken forgets that it makes very little difference what he believes in the matter, so long as the covenant-keeping God believes in pledges. The pledge is an institution that God has set up, and no man has a right to say he does not believe in it. Has God not promised to send his floods no more upon our earth, and set his rainbow signature to the pledge written across his heavens? Away back in the beginning of the ages God began his pledges; and long years afterward Paul, writing to the Galatians about it, said that even the law could not break the covenant which had been confirmed before of God, to make the promise of none effect."

In the silence that followed these impressively spoken sentences came the clear voice of the student member of the faithful few.

"I was noticing today," said he, "the theological definition of the word 'covenant.' It is this: 'The promises of God as revealed in the Scriptures, conditioned on certain terms on the part of man, as obedience, repentance, faith, etc.' So, then, a covenant, in distinction from a mere promise, implies a condition, and indicates that both parties are concerned in the keeping of it. It seems to me that the first sentence of our Christian Endeavor pledge gives it the nature of a covenant, 'Trusting in the Lord Jesus Christ for strength.' We do not make this pledge alone; it is not a promise to God that we will do certain things for his benefit, but rather an acceptance of his promise to give us strength to do his will. Our pledge then merely states the conditions we must fulfill in order to understand that will. Am I right, doctor?" and he turned loving eyes to his elder pastor's face as he sat down.

"Exactly so, my dear boy," said the old minister, as he rose again. "In signing your names to this pledge you merely do as Jacob did when he rose up and took a vow upon himself that he would do as God had told him to do, if God would keep his covenant. Even as Jacob set up the rock for a memorial to the mutual promise, so do you sign your names to these small white cards, which may have cost some of you wakeful nights, as Jacob's stone pillow cost him. More than this"—and as he spoke the voice of the old Christian veteran seemed to soften and grow tremulous—"there may be some of you who do not know that the supper of our Lord, the sign, the seal, the center of our religion, is, first of all, a covenant, a pledge. You know we call it the sacrament. Do you know the word is derived from the Latin *sacramentum?* And the *sacramentum* was the oath of allegiance of the Roman soldiers. When a new legion had been enlisted, it was the custom to perform the solemn ceremony of taking the *sacramentum*. A shield was taken, upturned, and into it were poured a few drops of the blood of each soldier and of their commander, which was collected from a slight gash made in the bared arm of each by his own sword. Then the shield was held aloft by the commander, and the soldiers passed by in turn, each one as he passed dipping his hand into the blood with the commander. By so doing captain and soldier swore fealty each to the other by this solemn symbol, the captain promising to stand by the soldier, and the soldier by the captain, even to the shedding of the last drop of blood. It was this spirit that made the Roman legion the finest military organization the world has ever seen. It is this spirit that breathes through every part of the communion, the sacrament. Dear young fellow-soldiers, never forget that the communion means the renewal of Christ's vow to you as well as yours to him. Without this, my sixty-seven years of service in Christ's cause could not have been. With this spirit, I pray, I believe, that the Christian Endeavor army, setting it forth so clearly as is done in their pledge, will recruit a legion before whose endurance and devotion to their Master the devotion and endurance of the famed Roman legion will pale. This is my idea of the purpose and the effect of the Christian Endeavor pledge." So saying, he sat down.

There was a hush over the meeting. The young man who had objected to pledges shrank into a small space behind a pillar, and tried to look careless while he read the hymnbook. The others were taking in for the first time the solemnity of their covenant vows. Some drew out their cards and read them, while others' eyes sought the large wall-roll containing, in clear lettering, the pledge. At last a conscientious one spoke.

"Mr. President," he said, "the pledge has always seemed a solemn thing to me, but I have objected to signing because it seemed to me I could not always be sure of keeping my promise. It is too much to promise that I will do whatever Christ would have me do, for how can I be sure in every case just what it is that he would have me do? And then those two things that follow—praying and reading the Bible every day. I do not like to promise that; for I might forget it some time, or there might be occasions or circumstances when it might be impossible. For instance, I have frequently come home from work quite late at night, when my evident duty was to go immediately to rest without taking time for protracted devotions. And what if one were traveling, detained on the road overnight, without a Bible? Or there might be many other circumstances under which one would be compelled to break such a promise. I do not like to promise something that I am not sure I can keep."

Then arose the earnest-faced secretary, who had always a ready answer.

"Mr. President, it seems to me that the rules of daily Bible reading and prayer, together with that first clause, 'Trusting in the Lord Jesus Christ for strength,' are for the purpose of helping us to know and decide under all circumstances just what Jesus Christ would have us do. If we ask his guidance, and read his Word, which is a lamp to light our way, and trust the Spirit to lead, how can we mistake the way that he would have us take? And if we remember the clause, 'I will make it the rule of my life,' which precedes the promise concerning the prayer and Bible reading, the tenderest conscience need not be afraid to promise."

"And I want to say," added a frank-faced member of the faithful few, "that I objected to signing the pledge once on that account. I said I was afraid I couldn't always get time to read the Bible; but I found out on looking into my heart that the true reason was that I did not want to tie myself to reading every day. Then I signed the card. I keep it in the frame of my dressing-case mirror, where I see it whenever I enter my room. I want to say right here that I have discovered one benefit of the pledge-card; many a time it has reminded me, and I have opened my Bible just because I promised, when otherwise I would have thought myself too tired or too busy to read, and I've found the bit of comfort, or rest, or admonition, that I exactly needed. I don't believe anyone is ever too tired or too busy to read at least one verse in the Bible every day, and he will surely find himself better off for doing so. It seems to me in these days of cheap Bibles that every Christian might have a small Bible or a piece of one in his pocket, so that it wouldn't be possible for us to get caught anywhere unable to keep that part of our pledge."

"The only thing I object to in the pledge," said a constitutional objector, "is the part about the regular church services. Of course I'll go to church when I can; and it seems to me an utterly unnecessary cumbering of the pledge. I must say if I go to the Christian Endeavor meeting, I consider I have done my duty, and I don't feel bound to go out to the Wednesday evening church prayer meeting, nor to stay to evening preaching Sunday if I want to go home. The fact is, I can't conscientiously spare so much time to meetings."

This brought the dear old pastor to his feet again.

"Children," he said, "dear children, now right here let me warn you. Don't make a mistake. The greatest argument that has ever been urged against the Christian Endeavor movement is that it draws the young people away from the church prayer meetings and regular church services, and that their hearts are enlisted merely for their society, and not for the church of Christ. Take care. That is right against the Christian Endeavor principles. Your motto is, 'For Christ and the Church.' What is your organization for, if not to do better work for and in the church? And how can you do it if you, who are to be its future members and pastors and leaders, go away from its meetings, and leave us poor old folks, who are almost ready to leave the church on earth for the one in heaven, to run all the meetings? We need you in our prayer meetings, and we need you in the church services, both morning and evening. Bring your short prayers and verses and speeches into the church prayer meeting, and help us old ones to be young. Bring your fresh, earnest faces to the evening service, to encourage the pastor as he preaches, and to help us to draw in outsiders. You can always conscientiously give that as a reason to your heavenly Father for absenting yourself from your own meetings."

"But these excuses," said another. "I'm not always willing to give to the world my reason for being away from meeting, and I don't like the idea of pledging to speak in meeting always. It makes the speaking or praying merely perfunctory. Why not leave that out, and let us take part when we have something to say?"

Said the chairman of the prayer meeting committee: "But how could we keep up the interest in our meetings if we were not sure the members would all be present, and would be sure to take some part? There would be times when no one would feel like saying anything; and if the pledge was taken away, many of the members would cease to make preparation before meeting. The excuse is but a help, after all, making the members and the meeting feel that they are in sympathy, even if they are not all able to be in one room at the meeting."

There was much discussion before this meeting finally broke up; but at its close many pledge-breakers came forward and re-signed the pledge, and others, who had never been interested before, came, asked for pledge-cards, and went home thoughtfully studying them.

The result was that in a few weeks the membership roll of the society had largely increased, the attendance was trebled, and there were added interest and solemnity in the meetings. The next week's Wednesday evening prayer meeting felt the change. Many young faces were there, and several young voices timidly broke the pauses which had hitherto been so painful. The weeks that succeeded proved that this was not a momentary prick of conscience which had been given to the society. The members took it upon themselves to see that there was a large delegation always at the church prayer meeting, and they urged upon every possible occasion the supremacy of the church service over their own society meeting. No more went the society trooping home or out to take a pleasant walk Sunday evening, instead of going into the church after their prayer meeting. It gladdened the hearts of both pastors to see the large audiences; and outsiders began to wonder what were the attractions in that church, and to come and see.

Nor was this all. Even the new assistant pastor had to acknowledge a spirit of willingness to help on the part of all his young people; and just about a year from that time his faithful few had that talk with him about the pledge, he gathered them all in a group about him after a sweet Sunday's work was done, and told them: "Dear friends, I want to take back what I said a year ago, for I have learned better things. I do believe in the Young People's Society of Christian Endeavor; and I do believe, for I have been made to see the value of it, in its pledge."

A MISSIONARY
MEETING

HAT'S the subject of our meeting to-night, Tom?" asked Cousin Helen one Sunday afternoon. "I've lost my topic card, and could not remember what was given out in church this morning; so I ran in here to see yours."

"It's an old missionary meeting," answered Tom, throwing down the paper he had been reading. "I wish it was anything else."

"Why, Tom Brainard! Aren't you ashamed of yourself?" said Helen, laughing at the expression on his face.

"I don't know as I am," answered Tom. "Sit down, Helen. I've been bothered about this ever since church was out. You see, Fred Millard is sick. It was his turn to lead; and he has sent word to me to lead it, and I can't find a thing on earth to make it go. You can't make a missionary meeting interesting, anyway. Just think back, Helen; we've never had one interesting missionary meeting in all the time our society has been organized, have we?"

"No," admitted Helen, after a moment's sober thought. "I don't know that we have."

"Well, just see; here it is the time of year when there'll be a good many strangers from the hotel present—that is, if our hotel committee has done its work well—and there ought to be a meeting that will do them good. We have grand ones when we have any other topic, but a missionary meeting just kills us dead. There'll be nothing but dry statistics, and every stranger that comes in will wish he had stayed at home. I don't know how to manage it, I'm sure. Dr. Brower will get up and read a long article from some magazine; and who will know any more when he is done than when he began? Then we'll sing 'From Greenland's Icy Mountains,' and 'Rescue the Perishing,' and there will be some more statistics read by Fannie Moore and Miss Van Anden, and then the meeting will drag. And what I'm to do for my part of it I'm sure I don't know"; and Tom slid down a little farther in his easy chair, and scowled.

Helen laughed at his description; but she felt that it was perfectly true.

"They are boring, that's a fact, Tom—or rather, always have been," she said; "but I don't see why they should be. If missionary meetings are good things to have—and I suppose they must be, or they would not be upheld by all the good people in the church, and urged so much by the head of our society —why, then there must be some way to make them interesting."

"I should like to know what it is," said Tom.

"How nice it would be if we only had a real missionary with us to talk about missions, wouldn't it?" said Helen thoughtfully.

"I don't know," said Tom gloomily; "we haven't, anyway, so what's the use? And if we had, he would be likely to tell just as many statistics as Dr. Brower will read. Besides, that wouldn't be what I should call a Christian Endeavor missionary prayer meeting. That would be more like a lecture, or an amusement for us, if it was at all interesting."

"That is true," answered Helen. "Well, if missionary work is one of the things that we as Christians ought to have to do with, and to help along in, why shouldn't we be interested in it as well as in any other subject?"

"Well, we aren't," said Tom almost crossly; "and I don't see how we are to get up an interest, I'm sure. As for professing to be interested in those long articles full of strange names of places and people, I can't say I am, and that's all there is about it. I never feel as if I had received a bit of good from them. I only wish *you* had to lead this meeting."

"Well, I don't," answered Helen, laughing, "for I should be as much at a loss as you are; but, Tom," and her face sobered, "have you been to the Head for orders?"

"What do you mean?" asked her cousin, with a puzzled expression.

"Why," said Helen, her cheeks growing a little pink, and hesitating, she hardly knew why, to speak what she had to say, "I mean, have you prayed about it?" She looked down in her lap, and fingered the corner of her handkerchief. These two cousins were used to talking about their society and all that pertained to it, but had always felt a little shy of speaking plainly about what was most dear to them. They lived next door to one another, and were dear companions on all occasions; but it was a little hard for Helen to say what she did.

Tom looked at her in surprise for a minute, and then laughed in a rather embarrassed way.

"No, I don't know as I have," he answered; "but what—well—what good would that do? God has given me brains; doesn't he expect me to do the best I can with them?"

"O Tom, you know better than that. You know he has told you to ask his help always; and hasn't he promised to even give words when they are needed? Why, it's his meeting, Tom, not yours; and he certainly doesn't want it to be an uninteresting one. He would like to have it reach the hotel strangers as much as you would. You ask him now, and I will run home and pray about it too"; and she started toward the door.

"No, wait, Helen!" he said, rising quickly, and catching her hand to detain her. "You stay here and pray. Let us pray together. We are not afraid of each other; and we can claim the promise that 'If two of you shall agree on earth as touching anything that they shall ask, it shall be done,' you know"; and he led her over to the sofa, where they both knelt and opened their hearts to God about the meeting that night.

As they arose, Tom said, "Now, Helen, you must stay and help me get ready," and so through the Sunday afternoon they studied. Papers and books were brought out; the missionary news columns were carefully looked over. The two young people grew quite excited over their work as the time went by and the hour of the meeting drew nearer.

"My, I wish I had a whole week to get ready in!" exclaimed Tom at last, as he threw down the pile of papers he had been looking through, and reached over to the table for his Bible.

"But you have enough items now that are interesting, Tom," said his cousin.

"Yes, enough, perhaps," admitted Tom; "but I would have liked to give them out to the members early in the week, and they would have been thinking about it, and have had a little word ready to add. It would have been a great deal better."

"And some of them would have been praying for the success of the meeting, too, perhaps, if their special attention had been called to it," added Helen gently.

"Perhaps," said Tom, "and, after all, that's the secret of a good meeting. But we must have some Bible now," and he plunged into his study of that. What a whirl he felt himself in then! There was enough Bible on the subject of missions to supply material for unnumbered meetings. Tom began to wonder why he had never discovered it before. What theme should he take? The thought of Christian giving? Shining as lights in a dark world? Witnessing for Christ? Helping Christ's kingdom to come? There were verses and verses, and they all rushed in upon him at once, and bewildered him.

"Helen," he said in desperation, "there won't be time for any items from the papers, as far as I can see; the Bible has too much to say about it. I had no idea this subject was so rich."

Helen looked up with flushed cheeks and shining eyes.

"O Tom! isn't it grand? We might have a missionary meeting every week for a year, and then not exhaust the subject. We shall just have to go over these bits we have cut from the paper, and drop out all but two or three of the very best, and that will leave room for more Bible."

"Yes; but Helen, what shall I do about selecting a passage to read? If I begin, I can't find a place to stop."

"Take the grandest one you can find, the one that will suggest the greatest number of other passages, and at the same time be the one that others would be the least likely to select," answered Helen.

The twilight found them still at work, but with more hopeful hearts than at first. A very few slips of neatly written paper represented their work that afternoon. On the papers were some items of interest concerning mission work, and a few carefully selected texts of Scripture, which the careless searcher would not be likely to find, these to be handed to one or two timid members who never knew what to say, especially on the subject of missions. Helen and Tom had planned just which ones they should be handed to, and had made the most of the talents of the people they knew would probably attend the meeting.

"There's Albert," said Tom. "No need to hand him anything; he'll be sure to have something good to say, even if the subject of the meeting should be, 'How to build church steeples.' "

"Yes," said Helen, "and so will Mary Elder; and I sometimes think that those two help more than any other two in our society, because what they say always makes one feel as if they lived very near to Jesus."

By and by the bell began to toll, and Tom and Helen walked down the street toward the church side by side. They were quiet now. They had just come from their own rooms, where each had spent a few minutes in earnest prayer for a blessing on the meeting; and as they entered the pleasant chapel, they breathed one more word of petition.

The room was filling rapidly already, and many strangers were among the number. The town was a small winter resort in the South, and this was the season of year when tourists were most numerous.

"Oh, isn't it just an awful pity that this is a missionary meeting?" whispered Clara Horton to another earnest follower of Jesus Christ. "Just see all these strangers, and they will be sure not to be interested. There goes that man who came in a private car three days ago. He stops at the hotel, and is very rich. They say he scarcely ever goes to church. I wonder what brought him. I didn't think the hotel committee would hardly dare send one of their invitations to him. He looks scornful. I just know he'll make all sorts of fun. It's too bad that it isn't a consecration meeting, or anything else but missionary night."

"Yes, it is a pity," assented her friend, glancing in the direction of the haughty looking, handsome old man who had been seated well up toward the front. "It's strange that he cared to come to a young people's meeting, isn't it? What a pity he couldn't have been here last week! We had such a good meeting then!"

The meeting was opened by singing; and the children of the heavenly Father who supposed themselves so wise stopped whispering to sing,

There's a work for me, and a work for you,
Something for each of us now to do.

They sung the words without thinking much what they were. It was an old hymn. Tom had hesitated when he selected it, but it seemed to fit so entirely into his thoughts that he could not but use it. His prayer that followed the hymn was one of personal consecration and of earnest pleading for the presence of Jesus in the room that evening; and the sharp old man eyed the young leader intently as he gave out another hymn, "One More Day's Work for Jesus," and sat down to turn over the leaves of his Bible a moment.

Tom read only two verses, after all, from the many that he had found. They were these: "The God of our fathers hath chosen thee, that thou shouldest know his will, and see that just One, and shouldest hear the voice of his mouth. For thou shalt be his witness unto all men of what thou hast seen and heard."

He said but few words himself. His thought was that each one of the members of that society was chosen of God as a missionary to do some special work, even though it might be but small.

"I have asked Miss Gladden to sing us an old song that illustrates this thought," he said in conclusion, as he nodded to the young lady at the organ.

It was not a wonderful voice that sang the words; but it was sweet and clear, and every word was spoken with a distinctness that brought it home to each heart listening:

Hark, the voice of Jesus calling,
"Who will go and work today?"

The sharp eyes of the old man watched the singer's face as she sang, and he cleared his throat several times at the close. The room was very still, hushed by the thought of the song, when Tom said, "Let us have a good many short prayers. John Raymond, will you lead us?" and immediately every head was bowed.

Oh, they were earnest Christians, every one of them, only they were not used to carrying their consecration into their missionary meetings. But now every heart was lifted up for a blessing, and they had all forgotten that this was a missionary meeting. There followed in quick succession many heartfelt sentences of pleading for blessing, of earnest consecration, and some even breathing the spirit of the answer to the Master's call, "Here am I, Lord; send me, if thou hast aught for me to do."

"Let us sing one verse" said Tom, when there came a pause, and they sang:

If once all the lamps that are lighted
  Should steadily blaze in a line,
Wide over the land and the ocean,
  What a girdle of glory would shine!
How all the dark places would brighten!
  How the mists would roll up and away!
How the earth would laugh out in her gladness,
  To hail the millennial day!
Say, is your lamp burning, my brother?
  I pray you, look quickly and see;
For if it were burning, then surely
  Some beam would fall brightly on me.

"The verse that we have just sung," said a young girl, "reminds me of what a returned missionary once told me. She said that she had always taught her little girl, who had been born in Turkey, and who had never been to this country, that America was a Christian land; and the little girl, without her knowledge, had formed the idea that everyone who lived here belonged to Jesus Christ and served him. When they brought her here she was about seven years old. One day her mother took her out in the street of a city, and in passing some men she heard them swear. The little girl stood looking after them sorrowfully, and then said to her mother, 'Mamma, I feel sick.' Her mother took her home as quickly as possible, and after she felt better questioned her as to what had happened that made her feel so ill all in a minute; for the mother thought her symptoms indicated that she had had a shock of some sort. 'Oh, Mamma,' she answered, 'you told me this was a Christian land, where everybody loved Jesus; and I heard some men use God's name in the way the bad men over in Turkey used to do.' The little trusting heart had evidently been shocked by finding that in this land where everyone knows about Jesus, not all were followers of him. If we would only, all of us whose lamps are lighted, go to work and keep our lights bright, might we not make a difference in this country, so that when those from lands that do not honor our God come over here, they will find that this is truly a Christian land? There is indeed much work left here for missionaries to do."

"I have been thinking," said one of the young men, standing up and facing the roomful of people, "while the sweet song was being sung to us, of Miss Havergal's poem:

In God's great field of labor
All work is not the same;
He hath a service for each one
Who loves his holy name.
And you to whom the secrets
Of all sweet sounds are known,
Rise up, for he hath called you
To a mission of your own."

Said Helen: "I have been interested in reading about a Christian Endeavor Society in a foreign land.

It is in a mission boarding school, and is formed of young men and women who have known Jesus Christ but a short time, most of them. They are very poor, as the mission board can appropriate but little to the needs of the school; and there are constantly scholars wishing to enter the school who cannot be allowed to do so, because there is no money to pay for even the barest necessities of life. The boys of the school go out to sell papers and such things on Saturdays, and so are able to earn a few cents to help along; but in that country it would be a disgrace for the girls to do the same, so they have very few ways of earning any money for themselves.

"There came a young man to the school one day, a friend of some of the other students, and begged to be allowed to enter as a pupil; but the teachers sadly shook their heads, saying, 'We cannot allow it. We have no money to feed you, and nothing with which to buy books for you, and we cannot afford to let you enter without paying the small tuition that is necessary to keep the school running.' The young man turned sadly away; but some of the scholars got together and talked it over, and it was brought up in their Christian Endeavor meeting. The result was that the whole society went to the teachers, and said, 'We have decided that we will give up our meat on Fridays [they were so poor they could afford to have meat but once a week] if you will take the money that buys the meat for us, and use it toward paying for this poor boy who wants to learn about Jesus Christ.' They were allowed to do so. Then the boys each gave what money they could earn in selling their papers, gladly sacrificing the little comforts they had been able thus to procure for themselves.

"But the girls said, 'What can we do? We cannot go out to sell things.' They got together and talked the matter over, and decided that they would go without their meals on one day out of every week if the money that supplied the table for that day could be used for the poor boy. It seemed to me, after reading that true story, that we in our society know nothing at all about sacrificing for missions, that those poor Christians have gone way ahead of us. If they can do so much, shall we hesitate over giving up some luxury?"

This seemed to touch many hearts, and brought out other items and thoughts.

"Ye have not chosen me, but I have chosen you, and ordained you, that ye should go and bring forth fruit, and that your fruit should remain: that whatsoever ye shall ask of the Father in my name, he may give it you," recited another member, adding, "My heavenly Father has frequently comforted me with that verse, reminding me that it is not my work, after all, that I am doing, but his, for which he has chosen me, and that however dark the way may seem, and however my plans may have come to naught, yet I have ever the assurance that the fruit shall remain; and, with that promise that whatever I shall ask of the Father shall be given, why need I doubt and grow discomfited when my plans for doing

his work seem for a time to fail? I want, as my blessing from this meeting, to get more faith in his service, and less trust in myself."

When the hour was over it was a surprise to all.

"We have had a good meeting!" exclaimed one and
another, as they looked into each other's astonished
eyes at the close, and shook hands with the warm
clasp that they always used when their hearts had
been touched.

But it was the haughty old man in the front seat
who gave the final surprise to the little society, and
started its enthusiasm for a new era of missionary
meetings. He stepped up to Tom as soon as the bene-
diction had been repeated, and laid his hand on
Tom's shoulder, while the other hand gave that
amazed young man a roll of bills.

"Give that to your treasurer for the missionary
cause," he said, and hastened away before Tom had
time to frame fit words of thanks.

Fifty dollars all at once to go into their missionary
fund! It was more than this little society had
dreamed of giving for years yet. They were poor,
and for the most part the money came in slowly and
in very small quantities. They gathered in a group
about Tom, looking with reverence at the bills. It
seemed to them a material sign that the Lord had
truly been with them that night and blessed them;
and those few who always stayed a few moments to
talk things over after the others were gone, went
home with the feeling that they could never have
another cold, dry, statistical missionary meeting
again.

"Helen," said Tom, as he reached out his hand to relieve her of her Bible and hymnbook, on their way home, "this has been a wonderful evening for me, and I believe it is all a credit to you. The Lord put it into your heart to suggest the praying. I do believe that has been the matter with all our meetings. There has not been enough of prayer—beforehand and during the meeting, too. I mean to do differently about that hereafter. That is the secret of success in Christian work, after all. It has helped us all this time, and I shouldn't wonder at all if the old man felt that he had a blessing, too. Prayer is a wonderful thing!"

SOME CAROLS
FOR THE LORD

ALF a dozen young people were on their way home from a Christian Endeavor social when the idea was first mentioned, and this was how it began.

"What are we going to do for Christmas as a society?" asked Jessie. "I wish we could think of something new and delightful."

"So do I," chimed in Kittie. "We have never done anything but just join with the Sunday school in having a Christmas tree. I'm tired of trees, for my part, though I suppose the little children like them. But there is such a lot of work, and not much to show for it afterward. We get all tired out fixing dolls, and deciding which child shall have a book, or which ought to have a ball. Then the children are often disappointed at what they receive, and the church is covered with popcorn and mashed candies, and you can't go there to service for a week or two afterward without finding an old nut or a gumdrop hiding somewhere under your seat, no matter how hard you sweep. I worked like a slave for three hours last year, helping to sweep the church the day afterward, and then kept finding stray candies and bits of gold paper for a month."

"You might have a fishpond," suggested Fred Hall.

"O Fred, don't!" groaned Jessie. "We want something new that we've never tried before. Fishponds are as old as the hills; and so are old women who lived in a shoe, and had so many children they didn't know what to do. Besides, I never did think those things were suitable for the church; and they make as much mess and work, and aren't nearly so dignified as a tree."

"I'm squelched, Jessie," laughed Fred; "and I retire from making any further suggestions."

"I wish we had the custom of singing Christmas carols in this country; I think it is so pretty," said Myrtle Brown.

"That's an idea!" exclaimed Jessie. "We might sing some. Wouldn't that be interesting?"

"I should like to know if that isn't 'old as the hills,' as you termed it, madam?" said Fred.

They all laughed, of course, and tried to explain to Fred the difference; and when the hubbub had somewhat subsided, Myrtle put in again, "We tried it once on a small scale, my three cousins and I. We were up in the country for the holidays; and we stole out of the house before anyone was awake, when it was scarcely light, and sang under the windows. It was a great deal of fun, and they said it sounded very sweet. I should think it might do good if we chose the right carols."

"It's just the thing!" exclaimed Jessie. "Let's do it. We could have two or three bands of singers, and divide the town, each band taking a district. I've heard of great good done through singing. We might reach some in that way that we have not been able to reach in any other. Who are we here, anyway? I'm chairman of the social committee; I shouldn't wonder if such things came among our duties. Myrtle, you and Kittie and Frank are all 'socials.' We're all here but Truman. Harold, you're chairman of the Sunday school committee, aren't you? And Fred—"

"Only your humble president," put in Fred before Jessie could finish, "and I'll try to forget my feelings and do anything that's expected of me."

They grew very eager with their laughing and talking. All were agreed that the plan was at least interesting. Each knew some pretty carol that he would like to have sung, and each had some suggestion.

"What'll you do with all the money we've been putting aside for a Christmas entertainment? You know we decided last Christmas to save some each month for Christmas, so that when the time came we would not have to run all over town, and use the children's collections, which they had been supposed to give for the heathen, in order to buy them dolls and kites and books and things. I shouldn't wonder if the youngsters would be disappointed too." This was Harold's contribution to the conversation.

"We might take the presents along, and tie them to the doorknobs," suggested Frank.

"That's a good thought," said Jessie, amid the laughter that followed this proposal.

"But, Jessie," said Myrtle, "we couldn't get enough things to go around, and some would be disappointed."

"Why, Myrtle, I'm not so sure of that," she responded seriously. "It wouldn't do for us to sing under the windows of any but our own church people, or of those who belonged to no church, and are not being got hold of by any other, because the other two churches would be sure to think we were proselyting. I should think we might get together enough things to go respectably around among the people who legitimately belong to our society. I don't mean members merely of the society and church, but people whom we ought to be able to get hold of, and have not been able to reach heretofore. We could at least leave a Christmas card at each door."

"That would be beautiful; but we should have to keep it a grand secret from those we were to sing to," said Myrtle.

"Let's go in and see if Dr. Clifton likes the idea. We can't do anything without his approval, and I can't wait until morning. I want to dream out more plans," said Jessie. "Isn't it good that the social was so far away tonight? We have things in really quite a presentable shape to talk about."

"I'm afraid it's too late tonight, Jessie," suggested Kitty prudently. But just then they came to the pastor's gate, and found him standing there himself, bidding good night to a gentleman.

"O Dr. Clifton! May we come in and tell you a new plan, and see if it's worth anything? It will not take long, and we can hardly wait till morning," exclaimed Jessie eagerly.

"Certainly, certainly; come in, friends. I shall be only too glad to hear it. I can't wait until morning myself; I'm all curiosity," said the genial old minister.

Of course he approved the plan; and it was with faces full of a delightful secret that they once more took their way home.

It was near the last of November, and there were many things to be done; but the workers were all eagerness. The president called a meeting of the society in haste, and stated to them that the social committee had a plan for Christmas which, in order to be carried out to perfection, must be kept a secret from all except those whom they should call to their aid. He further said that the pastor knew and approved it, and that the committee would like to be authorized to go forward and carry out their plans. The chairman of the committee then stated that a part of their plan was to have the usual amount of money spent in gifts, and that they should like to be allowed to use the sum that had been set apart for that purpose.

The question having been carried by vote, the chairman said that they should need the assistance of every member in the carrying out of their project, and that, as they wanted to begin work at once, they would ask the following members to go to the different Bible-class rooms as they were called. He then read the names in groups of five, six, or seven, assigning each group to a separate classroom of the church. Each one of these groups was presided over by someone who had previously been instructed. All were soon at work. The strictest secrecy was enjoined upon the carolers, who commenced practicing at once.

The social committee, with a few others, had worked hard before this meeting, planning which members should be in the different groups, and dividing the town into districts, that no time might be lost if their plan was accepted. There was much to be done yet. A large calling committee was started around to ascertain the number of people in each house that they intended visiting, their ages, tastes, needs, and desires. They were to use every means possible to find out in what way they could make most useful the little money they had to spend.

The pastor announced that the Christian Endeavor Society was preparing for a celebration at Christmas time, and would be glad of contributions of turkeys, vegetables, groceries, dry goods, toys, or anything that usually goes to make up Christmas festivities; and that for the convenience of the contributors they would be visited by the committee some time during the week.

The committees themselves were not to be told in what way the gifts were to be distributed until Christmas Eve. They rather enjoyed the mystery that hung about the affair; and matters went on more smoothly than they had ever gone before, because everyone, except the social committee, was in such absolutely blissful ignorance, that none could venture to demur at what was to be done and want it to be different.

It had been arranged that on Christmas evening there should be a Christmas service held in the church. This being generally known, it was supposed that any festivities of the occasion would take place at that time; and so the mind of the town was soothed to rest about the matter. The character of this meeting was not known exactly. That had been placed in the hands of others.

The time flew fast, as it always does when people have more than they know how to do. The night before Christmas arrived at last, and all the work was done. Baskets ticketed with the names of many people stood groaning with their heavy loads. There were turkeys and chickens and geese, rabbits and birds and beef; there were potatoes, Irish and sweet, cabbages, celery, cranberries, jellies, all the long list of things that make the best kind of a Christmas dinner. There were warm stockings and flannels and shawls, dress goods, some plain bits of finery, neat and pretty; toys, books, candy, nuts, popcorn, and Christmas cards. You could hardly mention a thing that ever has to do with Christmas that had not its representative in one of those baskets. The committees went to their beds tired, but with happy hearts. They had been told the secret of the whole plan the night before; and with sealed lips and dancing eyes each one went home rejoicing.

Several members were so burdened with the weight of their new secret that they were unable to sleep, and startled their respective families by lighting matches through the night, to see whether it was time to arise and begin. But nearly all the anxious parents were quieted to sleep at last; and the beautiful, sparkling Christmas Eve peacefully hastened its course, till at last the glittering stars, with their memories of a night long ago, began to pale, and the least faint streak of the Christmas morning appeared in the east.

Then those young people arose in haste, and, cautiously donning the apparel that they had been careful to put in a convenient place the night before, slipped down the stairs, and out of their several doors, holding in their hands, and munching on the way, the crackers that the leaders of the various choirs had insisted should be eaten before the work of the morning, or more strictly of the dawning, should be begun. It had been agreed that if any were late they should not be waited for, but the company should proceed to business exactly at the hour intended, and those who were late could follow and join them; but so eager were all these workers for the morning to come, that there were but two out of the whole number who were late, and those two joined their group before they had finished the first carol.

Waken, Christian children;
  Up, and let us sing
With glad hearts and voices
  Of our newborn King;

Up, 'tis meet to welcome
  With cheerful lay
Christ, the King of glory,
  Born for us today.

The clear voices rang out on the cold morning air, waking the sleepers to a new, glad day, startling some from dreams of sorrows to remember what they had almost forgotten, the true meaning of Christmas Day. While the carolers sang, the committees, made up of those who could not sing (or who thought they could not), deftly selected the turkey, or the dolls, or the Christmas cards, one or all, as the case might be, and tied them fast to the doorknob, making ready for the next house as the singers finished their verse and moved on.

At each house where they sang, in addition to the gifts, a small envelope addressed to the householder was left, containing a cordial invitation to him to attend, with his family, the "Christmas praise service," to be held that evening in the church. At the top of the card was printed, "Peace on earth, good will to men," and below the invitation these words, "For unto you is born this day a Saviour, which is Christ the Lord."

Some poor souls, on hearing the music, really felt for a moment that they must be in heaven, so sweetly did it ring out.

This is the winter morn
Our Saviour Christ was born,
Who left the realms of endless day
To take our sins away.

Have ye no carol for the Lord,
To sing his love, his love abroad?
Have ye no carol for the Lord,
To sing his love, his love abroad?
Hosanna! From all our hearts we raise,
Hosanna, Hosanna! And make our lives his praise.

It came to the houses of the rich, as well as the poor, this story sweet and old. There had been no respecting of persons that day. There were dainty cards with sprays of lovely flowers or bits of landscape and a sweet Bible verse for some, and there were a few copies of Professor Drummond's little white books, left where it was thought they might do good. The committee had taken great care in selecting and assigning gifts, and had really shown remarkable tact. There were some large houses where money indeed was adequate, but where love had been lacking long since, and where there had not been a Christmas gift in many a day. The gifts were gratefully received, how gratefully the society never knew in all cases, though they heard much about that Christmas Day in later days and years.

And the meeting that night? Why, of course, not everybody that was invited came, but many did. The church was crowded to overflowing. There was not even standing room left, despite the fact that in the two other churches of the town there were Christmas services at the same hour.

After the meeting had been opened by prayer, and singing of the good old Christmas hymn, "While Shepherds Watched Their Flocks by Night," there were several lovely Christmas solos, an exquisite recitation appropriate to the evening, and the reading of a short, touching story. Then an invitation was given for all to take part in the meeting who felt that they had anything to be thankful for. Five minutes were given to the recitation of Bible verses about the Prince of Peace and King of Glory, and Christmas and praise. How the verses came from all over the house! The strangers looked on in astonishment, some of them taking part. It had not seemed to them that there could be so many wonderful verses in the whole of the Bible. And then, in still more wonder, they bowed their heads and heard from many lips short sentences of prayer filled with praise to God and of pleading for forgiveness and consecration. There was time for a few words of testimony before they closed; and the testimonies came from all over the house again, and especially from those who had been benefited by the visits of the young workers in the morning.

"It's been the best Christmas we ever spent!" exclaimed the young people as they went home, still feeling the pressure of gratitude from many hands. "They'll come again; We know they will."

And they did.

THE PRAISE
OF MEN

*I*T was late, and Nellie Beverly was tired. She didn't feel much like reading her Bible; and yet there in the frame of her mirror, staring at her as she reached out her hand to turn off the gas, was her Christian Endeavor pledge. Its words, "to pray and to read the Bible every day," reminded her now that she had failed to keep her promise for that day, and, indeed, for the week before. The thought arrested her motion, and made her reach, instead, for her Bible that lay on its little stand by the dressing table. It was trying, this pledge, always bringing her up standing with its solemn phrases. She drew her brows together as she opened the Bible at random, intending to catch at a verse anywhere in order to satisfy her conscience. She had been one of those in her society who had objected to the good old iron-clad pledge; and, when she found it was inevitable, had argued for some time that the sentence about Bible-reading should be left out, on the ground that there were often times when it was impossible, or at least very inconvenient, to read the Bible every day, as when one was on a long journey, for instance. When that arrangement had failed, she had even debated with herself as to whether she would sign the pledge at all. It had ended in her finally signing; but the sight of that pledge-card always gave her an uncomfortable feeling lest she might not be living up to her vows.

Why was it that the Bible opened just where it did? She was not in the least superstitious, at least not about religion. There had been occasions, however, when it had marred her pleasure to make one of thirteen at the table, and she never counted the carriages at a funeral, and always took pains to see the new moon over her right shoulder. But she was not looking for any special word to be given that night, as she hurriedly scanned the pages with sleepy eyes to find a verse that looked short.

Her thoughts had been busy, too, even as she opened her Bible, with the occurrences of the evening. She had been taking part in an entertainment arranged by the social committee of their Christian Endeavor Society. Over in one corner of her room now was a large valise, which contained her different costumes and the many little things that it had been necessary for her to carry to the hall. Her parts had been difficult, and she had done well. Every one said so; and, indeed, she knew it herself without being told. She had been obliged to pose for several minutes in a difficult attitude, and had been applauded for the beauty and grace of the position, as well as for the steadiness of nerve and muscle shown. The classical costume she had worn was becoming, and there had been many admiring glances cast at her, in addition to more openly expressed admiration and showers of compliments given her. Mrs. Elihu Barker had offered to take her home in her carriage too; and her handsome young son, who had just returned from a German university, had opened the carriage door, helping her in, and seating himself beside her for the homeward ride. Her eyes shone with pleasure as she thought of his elegant compliments; she even felt a little pity for the other girls who had not enjoyed this distinction. To be sure, young Mr. Barker had sneered somewhat at the Christian Endeavor Society and its prayer meetings, and a few of his jokes and gracefully told stories had verged a little too much on the sacred to be altogether pleasing to this young woman who had named the name of the Lord and called herself his child. Nevertheless, she had laughed, for the jokes were exceedingly funny; and a young man who had spent so many years abroad was not expected to have exactly the same strict views of everything that were held here at home. He was very nice, and he had admired her. Vistas of pleasures seemed opening before her.

But what was this that her eyes were reading? "For they loved the praise of men more than the praise of God." Nellie felt startled as she read the words once more. How very strange for her to have opened to that verse! Did God mean to reprove her?

She had been thinking a good deal about herself during the last few weeks; and much time and expense had been put upon her preparations for the entertainment, in order that she might gain this "praise of men." It was true that she had been trying to make the entertainment a success for the sake of the society and to give pleasure to others; but really in her heart these things had been secondary, and her main thought had been, How shall I dress and act and pose and sing so as to excite the greatest amount of admiration? This was a rather ugly verse to pillow her head upon for the night. She liked to sink into sleep with the feeling that she had her heavenly Father's blessing; and this verse gave her an uncomfortable feeling, as if he were not altogether pleased with her. It seemed as if he had spoken the words in her ear. What did the verse mean, anyway? She did not remember ever to have seen it before. Who was it that loved to be praised so much? She read the verse before: "Nevertheless, among the chief rulers also many believed on him; but because of the Pharisees they did not confess him, lest they should be put out of the synagogue; for they loved the praise of men more than the praise of God."

With some impatience she ran her eye down the page to find, if she could, a pleasanter verse; and there, a little farther on, stood out the one that she had read in the prayer meeting last week, outlined in pencil that she might easily distinguish it then: "For I have given you an example, that ye should do as I have done to you."

Somehow the two verses had linked themselves together inseparably. This last one reminded her of how Christ had lived and died for her sake, of how he had borne shame, and how, when he was reviled, he opened not his mouth. The whole Book of Isaiah and all of the Gospels stood up with testimony for him in an instant; and there, on the other hand, was pictured in her mind her own behavior that evening, and all the thoughts and ambitions that had been in her mind. These thoughts did not please her, but she could not avoid them. She tried to argue with herself that she had not been so very wrong or vain, and that Mr. Barker was not a Pharisee, but a member of the church—at least, he had been before he went abroad. But she was obliged to go back to those first verses once more. How would it sound if a Bible of today were to be written, and the stories of the disciples of today were put down? Would this story of her own behavior read something like this, she wondered: "Nellie Beverly also believed on Christ; but because of Harold Barker and his set she did not confess him, lest she should be put out of society; for she loved the praise of men more than the praise of God"?

Nellie shivered at this. She had not intended to read all that into the Bible for her own benefit. Her mind had gone on in spite of her, and put the hateful thought into Bible phraseology. She shut the book hastily, and turned the gas out with a click, kneeling beside her bed, as was her custom. But her face was burning with shame as she hid it in her hands and tried to utter a feeble word or two of prayer.

She had thought but a few minutes before that it would not take her long to be asleep that night; but when she laid her head down, after praying, she could not go to sleep for a long time. She had much thinking to do. She must examine her life, and decide what the future should be. She was suddenly brought face to face with her own vows, solemnly made and carelessly broken, and she was resolved that there should be a change. Now that her eyes were once opened, it took but a few minutes to decide what changes must be made in order that she might have the praise of God rather than the praise of men. God himself seemed almost to speak to her, and to show her clearly what her path ought to have been in the past.

It was on the next day that young Mr. Barker called; and Nellie, with a quiet lifting of her heart in prayer for help that she might be worthy of her high calling, went down to receive him. It gave her a little flutter of pleasure as he handed her a note from his mother, begging her to read it and report her answer to him. The note was gracefully worded, saying that guests from a distant city were to be with them over Sunday, and that Mrs. Barker was desirous that her young friend should meet them; and she wished also that they might hear her voice, which had delighted them all so much the evening before. Would Nellie give them the pleasure of her company at tea on Sunday evening, and do them the favor to bring some of her music with her? It could be something suitable for Sunday, of course.

There was an unmistakable glow of delight in

Nellie's eyes as she read this note. She had not expected to be taken right into intimacy in this delightful way by a family who moved in the highest circles of society. She raised her eyes to Harold Barker, who, scarcely giving her time to read the note, had gone on to tell her how delighted his mother was with her voice.

"And you should have heard the praise my uncle gave you, Miss Beverly," he was saying. "He considers your voice really remarkable, and I assure you he is a judge."

Sweet words these were to the girl who had spent so much time and money on her voice. But suddenly, as if a voice had spoken in her ear, came the words, "For they love the praise of men more than the praise of God."

Her face changed quickly. She heard no more of the handsomely turned sentences. All at once she became aware of a silence, following a question that had been asked her. She felt, rather than knew, that the question was with regard to her acceptance of the invitation.

"I am very sorry, Mr. Barker," she stammered out. "It would give me great pleasure to meet your mother's guests, and to sing for them, but it is on Sunday night, you know."

He hastened to assure her that he understood that she was not in the habit of going out on Sunday socially, but this was merely among themselves, very quiet. His mother had spoken of that, and said that she was not sure that Miss Beverly might not have some scruples on that account, and that she would have asked her for some other evening but for the fact that the friends were to leave them early Monday morning, and that all the evenings between this and that were fully occupied with other engagements. His mother was very anxious to have her come, and so, indeed, was he; and he hoped she would waive her objections for that time and come to them.

Nellie was not used to arguing on such subjects. She looked down in troubled silence during this speech, almost ready to yield, when the words of the pledge-card came to her mind as they had looked, framed in her mirror, the night before. Was it the Master's help that was given her through the wording of that pledge-card? She gathered courage, and spoke once more, "Mr. Barker, it is impossible. Our Christian Endeavor meeting comes very soon after the time your mother has named as your tea hour."

"Oh!" said he, "I was not aware that you were a member of that society." There was something in his tone that made Nellie remember all the bright sarcasms of the evening before with regard to the society. "But, really, Miss Beverly," more seriously, "I don't suppose you are bound by iron-clad laws to attend that special meeting, are you? Can you not forego the pleasures of your society for this once?"

Her cheeks grew still redder as she answered quietly, "I have promised, Mr. Barker; that is one of the pledges we make when we join the society, to attend the prayer meetings. I wish your friends were to be here longer, for I should enjoy meeting them. I am very sorry."

"But are there no conditions, Miss Beverly?" he asked, with an impatient frown on his handsome face. "Surely, you are not bound so hopelessly."

"Yes, there are conditions," she answered with a thoughtful, serious look; "the pledge reads, 'Unless hindered by some reason which I can conscientiously give to my Lord and Master.' Do you think that he would accept my own pleasure as an excuse for my staying away from a meeting when he himself has promised to be there?"

Harold Barker was fairly embarrassed, and did not attempt any answer, but looked at her in utter amazement. Surely, this could not be the same young lady who laughed and joked with him last night! He could not but respect her the more, however. She did not look in the least like an "enthusiast," or a "fanatic," or a "crank," or any of those individuals whom he had scornfully denounced. This was a new type of girl, he decided, or else America had changed greatly during his stay abroad. Could it be possible that this Christian Endeavor Society about which such a furor was being made was the cause of all this?

His call did not last much longer. There was nothing left for him to say upon the subject in which he was interested, and he did not know how to converse easily upon this new topic.

Nellie Beverly sighed a little as she thought of all the pleasures that she had put away from her. Her chance for attending those delightful receptions that Mrs. Barker was said to give was entirely over. Nevertheless, she went about her morning duties with a joy in her heart such as she had not known before. Up in her room once more she read over her pledge-card, and smiled at the last sentence, remembering that the next Sunday was the evening for the regular consecration meeting. More than all other meetings she would not have wished to miss this one. How would it have sounded, thought Nellie, if she had sent word to the society that she was obliged to be away from the meeting in order to take tea with some delightful musical and literary people at Mrs. Barker's?

The next Sunday evening proved to be a beautiful one; and the meeting was a solemn one, in which many pledged anew their lives and all to Christ. When Nellie Beverly's name was called, she read the two verses that had so moved her a few evenings before, and added, "I wish to learn to live for the praise of God, rather than the praise of men."

As she turned to lay aside her hymnbook at the close of the meeting, she saw Harold Barker just behind, watching her intently; and as their eyes met, he gave her a grave, respectful bow.